PICARD
NO MAN'S LAND

STAR TREK™
PICARD

NO MAN'S LAND

The script of the thrilling original audio drama

Kirsten Beyer
&
Mike Johnson

Based upon *Star Trek*
created by Gene Roddenberry
and
Star Trek: Voyager
created by
Rick Berman & Michael Piller & Jeri Taylor
and
Star Trek: Picard
created by
Akiva Goldsman & Michael Chabon
&
Kirsten Beyer & Alex Kurtzman

GALLERY BOOKS
New York   London   Toronto   Sydney   New Delhi

G

Gallery Books
An Imprint of Simon & Schuster, LLC
1230 Avenue of the Americas
New York, NY 10020

This book is published by Gallery Books, a division of Simon & Schuster, LLC, under exclusive license from CBS Studios Inc.

First Gallery Books trade paperback edition September 2024

GALLERY BOOKS and colophon are registered trademarks of Simon & Schuster, LLC

Simon & Schuster: Celebrating 100 Years of Publishing in 2024

For information about special discounts for bulk purchases, please contact Simon & Schuster Special Sales at 1-866-506-1949 or business@simonandschuster.com.

The Simon & Schuster Speakers Bureau can bring authors to your live event. For more information or to book an event, contact the Simon & Schuster Speakers Bureau at 1-866-248-3049 or visit our website at www.simonspeakers.com.

Interior design by Kathryn Kenney-Peterson

Printed and bound by CPI (UK) Ltd, Croydon CR0 4YY

10   9   8   7   6   5   4   3   2   1

Library of Congress Cataloging-in-Publication Data has been applied for.

ISBN 978-1-6680-6613-3
ISBN 978-1-6680-6614-0 (ebook)

STAR TREK™

PICARD

NO MAN'S LAND

ACT ONE

EXT. RAFFI'S TRAILER - PORCH - LATE NIGHT
CUE: SOULFUL SPANISH GUITAR

From inside the trailer, sounds of dishes and a
crash.

> RAFFI:
> You okay in there, Seven?

> SEVEN:
> (from the "kitchen")
> How long has your recycler been on the fritz?

> RAFFI:
> Uhhh...a decade, maybe?

Seven joins Raffi on the porch.

> SEVEN:
> That explains a great deal. These two are now
> clean.

> RAFFI:
> The red one is actually a bud vase.

> SEVEN:
> Oh.

> RAFFI:
> Give it here.
> (opens wine)
> I don't really do...clean.

> SEVEN:
> I'm not judging, Raffi. I get the appeal of
> this place.

> RAFFI:
> Lemme guess. The spacious accommodations? No—
> the homey, lived-in vibe?

Seven laughs.

> SEVEN:
> I was going to say, the solitude. It feels like no one has ever been here before or will be again.

> RAFFI:
> I'll drink to that. To you and me...

> SEVEN:
> ...and the middle of nowhere.

They toast.

> SEVEN (CONT'D):
> This is the last of the Château Picard.

> RAFFI:
> I know a guy. I'll call him tomorrow.

> SEVEN:
> Do you ever think about him rambling around that huge château? Alone.

> RAFFI:
> Plenty of people work there. But he's pretty good at alone.

> SEVEN:
> I noticed.

Raffi gets back to their game.

> RAFFI:
> Okay, my turn.

> SEVEN:
> That wasn't my question.

>   RAFFI:
> It ended with a question mark. Your voice
> lilted.

>   SEVEN:
> Oh, come on.

>   RAFFI:
> Plus, I already gave you a pass on the
> replicator question.

>   SEVEN:
> Fine.

>   RAFFI:
> First kiss?

>   SEVEN:
> Before or after I was severed from the
> Collective?

>   RAFFI:
> Wait—the Borg have sex?

>   SEVEN:
> That's two questions. You lilted.

>   RAFFI:
> Damn it.

>   SEVEN:
> First kiss was Axum.

>   RAFFI:
>   (intrigued)
> Axum? Borg or not Borg?

>   SEVEN:
> The relevant question would be conscious or
> unconscious. My turn.

                    RAFFI:
Hang on. You can't just throw that out there
and then—

                    SEVEN:
My turn. First crush?

                    RAFFI:
Ooooh, what was her name?

                    SEVEN:
I'm waiting.

                    RAFFI:
Uh...we were in school together. She was
fierce as hell.

                    SEVEN:
Still waiting.

                    RAFFI:
Jayna! I haven't thought about her in ages.
She broke my heart. Eleven-year-old me was a
mess.

                    SEVEN:
Eleven-year-old me was a Borg.

                    RAFFI:
Wow, that sucks. But it's still my turn—
conscious or unconscious?

                    SEVEN:
Depends on your definition of unconscious.
Axum was a drone I met from time to time
while regenerating.

                    RAFFI:
Isn't that the Borg version of sleep? Wait,

that wasn't my question, but dream kisses
don't count.

>   SEVEN:
> Oh, he was real. Some of us had a mutation
> that allowed us to access one another's
> consciousness in a shared thought space while
> we were regenerating. We were ourselves
> there. Not Borg. It was kind of beautiful,
> really.

Raffi bursts out laughing.

>   RAFFI:
> Do you have any idea how messed up that is?

Seven joins her.

>   SEVEN:
> I know. It really was.
>   (beat)
> I like this song.

>   RAFFI:
> Me too. Rios has got some great stuff here.
> Of course, he made it very clear the record
> player is a loan, on account of I need to
> expand my musical palate. Which is a pot/
> kettle situation for sure. Like everything
> Rios, most of these tend toward the "no one
> understands my existential pain" end of the
> spectrum.

>   SEVEN:
> I prefer not to wallow.

>   RAFFI:
> I spent too long overachieving in that
> department to throw stones.

SEVEN:
I had a friend who used to say, "Pain is inevitable, but suffering is optional."

RAFFI:
Bet she was a hoot at parties.

SEVEN:
He. And not really.

RAFFI:
He. Was he a good friend? More than a good friend?

SEVEN:
There was a time I thought maybe, but no.
            (beat)
I'm assuming you and Gabe's father were more than friends.

RAFFI:
Yes. For a very long time. Jae's an artist. High-end pieces. The kind of stuff that breaks you open and touches your soul before you even know what hit you.

SEVEN:
So, not Starfleet?

RAFFI:
Hell, no. The only thing harder than loving a civilian is making it work with a fellow officer.

SEVEN:
How long ago did that end?

RAFFI:
Pretty sure the recycler was still working.

SEVEN:
And since then?

RAFFI:
Oh, you know. A thing, here and there. Nobody
special.

SEVEN:
I'm sorry to hear that.

RAFFI:
Why?

SEVEN:
You deserve special.

RAFFI:
Aww, so do you.
          (beat)
Biggest regret.

SEVEN:
Don't have any.

RAFFI:
None?

SEVEN:
I don't do regret.

RAFFI:
Huh. On the one hand—badass. On the other—
seriously?

SEVEN:
Waste of time. Me again. Worst breakup?

RAFFI:
Probably Starfleet.

                    SEVEN:
Really?

                    RAFFI:
That surprises you?

                    SEVEN:
Yeah. You don't strike me as someone who
needs anyone.

                    RAFFI:
I don't?

                    SEVEN:
Would you go back if they'd have you?

                    RAFFI:
They won't. Bridges burned. Earth salted and
all that. But it's like a damned reflex. The
club everyone wants to join. By the time you
start to see the cold, hard reality of it,
it's too late. You're already in love. And
that love dies hard.
           (beat)
My turn.

                    SEVEN:
Is it? I'm kind of losing track.

                    RAFFI:
What do you want?

                    SEVEN:
Right now?

                    RAFFI:
Right now.

Wind rises.

                    SEVEN:
    This. Just this.

                    RAFFI:
    Come here.

Seven leans in to kiss Raffi.

A Fenris Ranger ship approaches.

                RAFFI (CONT'D):
    The hell is that? Nobody ever comes here.

                    SEVEN:
    You have weapons?

                    RAFFI:
    Is wine wet?

                    SEVEN:
    Not good wine.

Raffi gets weapons.

                SEVEN (CONT'D):
    Why is my rifle smaller than yours?

                    RAFFI:
    Newer model. Regenerative power cells.

                    SEVEN:
    I withdraw my objection.

Ship roars closer, and Raffi shouts over the
engine sound.

                    RAFFI:
    Any idea who that is?

The ship lands.

                    SEVEN:
    Yeah. Sorry. They're here for me.

EXT. RAFFI'S TRAILER - PORCH - LATE NIGHT

As the engine sound fades, the ship's captain, Hyro, approaches and addresses himself entirely to Seven, ignoring Raffi.

> HYRO:
> Miss Seven, glorious to see you as always, if you'd come with me, time is epigrammatic. Tempus fugitive and all that.

> RAFFI:
> I'm sorry, what now?

> HYRO:
> Your comms appear to be malfunctioning again. Perhaps a bit too much mayonnaise in the array manifold?

> RAFFI:
> Mayonnaise?

> SEVEN:
> I turned my comms off, Hyro.

> HYRO:
> Has a fulsome and lasting peace been declared throughout the former confuted territories?

> SEVEN:
> Not that I'm aware.

> HYRO:
> (simultaneous with Seven below)
> Because surely such a mountainous turn of events

> SEVEN:
> Get off my back. It's only been a few days.

HYRO (CONT'D):

would have been reported on the local news
feeds.

RAFFI:

So help me, if the both of you don't shut the
hell up for a second...

Silence.

RAFFI (CONT'D):

Thank you.

HYRO:

And who might this enchanting creature be?

RAFFI:

Raffi. Raffaela Musiker. Lieutenant
Commander. Former.

HYRO:

Could you just pick one of those and let me
know...

RAFFI:

Seven?

SEVEN:

Raffi, this is Hyro. Hyro, Raffi.

HYRO:

Delegated to make your acquaintance.

SEVEN:

Hyro's a Ranger. He was born on Nemulia.
Federation Standard isn't his native
language.

RAFFI:

Which is why we have universal translators.

                        SEVEN:
Please, don't get him started.

                        HYRO:
Universal translators? Never touch the
things. Most divisive, couthless contraption
known to sensitive life. To really understand
another culture, once must immerse oneself
completely in the most grain-like motes of
their language. So much of the truth, the
laminated beauty...

                        SEVEN:
Luminous.

                        HYRO:
...luminous beauty of a people begins with
the spoken word.

                        RAFFI:
Okay. But mayonnaise?

                        HYRO:
Oh, right. That's the dessert topping. I
meant...

                        SEVEN:
Trans-lubrisol.

                        HYRO:
Of course. Yes. Good. There it is.

                        RAFFI:
Hyro...was it? It's the middle of the night
and this is my property.

                        HYRO:
Abject apologies. Fenris Rangers don't really
keep normal business hours.

SEVEN:

Hyro.

HYRO:

Shall I return at a more opportune moment, one that doesn't interfere with your busy schedule?

SEVEN:

I just needed some time.

HYRO:

Ah, I see. I have conspicuously inserted myself into a personal moment.

RAFFI:
            (simultaneous with Seven below)
Yes.

SEVEN:

No.

Pause. They each clock their different responses.

RAFFI (CONT'D):
Oh. Well, then.

SEVEN:

Raffi, I didn't mean...

HYRO:

Dear gods, Ebla is going to be obliterated before you two get your story straight.

SEVEN:

What?

HYRO:

Rynin's back. And he's headed for Ebla.

                    SEVEN:
Shit. How'd he find it?

                    HYRO:
We don't know.

                    SEVEN:
The defense grid will hold.

                    HYRO:
It might have. But he's recently acquired a
gently used warbird. *D'deridex* class.

                    SEVEN:
Fully armed?

                    HYRO:
Feels like a safe assumption.

                    SEVEN:
Right.

                    RAFFI:
Rynin? Bastard son of Romulan senator
Pomarka?

                    HYRO:
Generally unpleasant, certainly, but...

                    RAFFI:
"Bastard" as in illegitimate. His mother was
never officially recognized by the Romulan
caste.

                    HYRO:
Huh. Do you know him?

                    RAFFI:
I was ten years Starfleet Intelligence,
Romulan division, and Pomarka made plenty

of enemies. Since when is his pissant kid
threatening anybody?

                    SEVEN:
Since the Neutral Zone collapsed and every
Romulan who can find a ship and crew wants to
reunite the empire under their banner. It's a
damn free-for-all out there these days.

                    HYRO:
And as we speak that...tiny bug...no, what
did you call him?

                    RAFFI:
Pissant.

                    HYRO:
Ah, what a delightful turn of phrase. Do you,
by any chance, know its entomology?

                    RAFFI:
How do you even function in the universe?

                    SEVEN:
How long?

                    HYRO:
Beg pardon?

                    SEVEN:
How long until Rynin reaches Ebla?

                    HYRO:
Days. If we're lucky.

                    SEVEN:
Damnit.

INT. RAFFI'S TRAILER - LATER

Raffi cleans up, at a loss for how to process this moment.

Enter Seven.

> RAFFI:
> Why are you still here?

> SEVEN:
> I'm sorry, Raffi.

> RAFFI:
> Somebody's in trouble. They need you. You gotta go. Right? Look, I knew this would happen. I just didn't think it would be so soon.

> SEVEN:
> Raffi.

> RAFFI:
> It's fine. I get it. I totally get it. Next time you're in the sector, look me up.

> SEVEN:
> Raffi, listen. When things started heating up on Romulus, there were people who knew what was coming and tried to get ahead of it. Museums, libraries, some priceless personal collections, basically as much of the cultural history of Romulus that could be packed in cargo ships was taken to Ebla and hidden behind a defense grid.

> RAFFI:
> I seem to remember a bunch of thefts reported back in the early days of the relocation.

                    SEVEN:

We weren't stealing anything. The artifacts
were given to the Rangers to protect.

                    RAFFI:

In whose name?

                    SEVEN:

History's. Civilization's. And many of their
former owners.

                    RAFFI:

Where is Ebla, anyway? How come I never heard
of it?

                    SEVEN:

Because you weren't supposed to. It's a tiny
world in a backwater system that's always
been marked as uninhabitable.

                    RAFFI:

That's—amazing, actually.

                    SEVEN:

I could use some help.

                    RAFFI:

Me? No. I'm not Ranger material.

                    SEVEN:

Neither are most of the people we work with.
They hear about us, show up for a mission
or two, and when they find out how bad the
conditions are and how crappy the pay is,
they move on. There's no pressure, no secret
handshake, no uniforms. You just go where
you're needed when you can.

Raffi stops cleaning and gives Seven her
undivided attention.

                        RAFFI:
It's a nice thing you're about to do. Like I
said, I respect you guys. But...

                        SEVEN:
Don't do it for me. Several thousand men,
women, and children live on Ebla. All of
them, and enough antiquities to fill a dozen
heavy cargo carriers, have to be moved
off that planet before Rynin arrives and
taken somewhere safe. You know anyone who
specializes in that kind of mission?

                        RAFFI:
That was a long time ago.

                        SEVEN:
Been longer since I met anyone worth doing
dishes for.

                        RAFFI:
My turn. You don't strike me as someone who
stays in one place very long. And I'm not
judging either.

                        SEVEN:
What's the question?

                        RAFFI:
Why do you want me to come along?

                        SEVEN:
I don't want walking out that door to be the
first thing I ever regret.

Long pause.

                        RAFFI:
When you say the pay is crappy, just how
crappy are we talking about?

INT. *TENDU* - BRIDGE - EARLY MORNING
CUE: CLASSIC ROCK TRACK

Raffi enters the bridge.

> RAFFI:
> Are you sure the music is loud enough?

> HYRO:
> Just getting into proper prelaunch spirit.
> Welcome to the fair ship *Tendu*.

> RAFFI:
> Sorry?

> HYRO:
> Deet? DEET?

Abruptly, the music ends.

> HYRO (CONT'D):
> Thank you, Deet. Miss Raffaela is joining us
> and clearly finds fun intolerable.

> RAFFI:
> What's a Deet?

> HYRO:
> Not what. Who. Deet? Stand up so our newly
> acquired killer of joy—I mean friend of
> Seven's—can see you.

Deet (very short male Okaran, 20s) rises. His
voice is a squeaky babble of syllables.

> DEET:
> [TRANSLATION: Hello, it is a pleasure to meet
> you, very tall human female.]

> RAFFI:
> Deet?

                    HYRO:
Never met a finer pilot.

                    RAFFI:
          (dubious)
How old is Deet?

                    HYRO:
Always thought it would be rude to ask. Is it
relevant?

                    DEET:
[TRANSLATION: She's beautiful, Hyro. Don't
scare her away.]

Hyro pretends to translate.

                    HYRO:
Old enough to know when he's being insulted
by a Starfleet prick.

                    DEET:
          (irritated)
[TRANSLATION: I didn't say she was a prick.
Stop it, Hyro.]

Suddenly, to everyone's surprise, Raffi replies
to Deet in his language—a little haltingly, but
understandable to Deet.

                    RAFFI:
          (the words "Deet" and "asshole" are
          said clearly)
[TRANSLATION: Nice to meet you, Deet.
Surprised a man as sharp as you can't find
work with someone who's isn't such an
asshole.]

                    DEET:
[TRANSLATION: Tough times all around.]

RAFFI:
I feel you. Great taste in music, by the way.
Just try to keep it a little below human-
eardrum shattering, okay?

DEET:
(happy)
[TRANSLATION: No problem.]

HYRO:
You speak...

RAFFI:
A little. Had a contact for years on
Freecloud who only spoke Okaran. Our UT could
never really parse it. Good guy. Drank me
under the table one time too many. But always
honest.

HYRO:
Not even a little surprised by that antidote.

RAFFI:
Nope.

HYRO:
Antipode?

RAFFI:
Not even close.

HYRO:
Anti...establishment?

RAFFI:
Why don't you just live with the mystery?

HYRO:
And you think I'm an asshole?

                    RAFFI:
Prove me wrong. How many ships are going to
be joining us at Ebla?

                    HYRO:
Won't know until we get there.

                    RAFFI:
What are their standard weapon systems like?
Who's coordinating tactical?

                    HYRO:
Until the engagement begins, we will live
with the mystery.

                    RAFFI:
          (gobsmacked)
I just...I really...

Seven enters the bridge.

                    SEVEN:
So? We're all friends now?

                    RAFFI:
          (simultaneous with Hyro below)
Um...

                    HYRO:
Well...

                    SEVEN:
Great, because we've got work to do. C'mon,
Raffi, our quarters are this way.

The ship powers up and launches from the surface.

INT. EBLA COMM CENTER
CUE: ADVENTURE THEME FADES INTO
MALE VOICE SINGING AND HUMMING

Professor Gillan (elderly) approaches Tyras (30s,
female Romulan) in mid-conversation with Pira
(20s, female Vulcan).

> GILLAN:
> (singing)
> *My darling, please remember all the good*
> *times we shared, because we'll be together*
> *again.*

> TYRAS:
> The first cargo containers are loaded and
> waiting on the transport platforms.

> PIRA:
> As soon as the first carriers arrive—

> GILLAN:
> (interrupting)
> Ah, Tyras. There you are. Where have all the
> fresh berries gone? Did you know that in
> Yamatath's high colonial period the prush
> berry was used as parchment ink?

> TYRAS:
> Professor Gillan, good morning. I'm sorry,
> but now isn't a good time...

> GILLAN:
> (to Pira)
> And who is this?

> TYRAS:
> This is Pira. She's coordinating our
> evacuation.

                    PIRA:
It is an honor to meet you, Professor Gillan.

                   GILLAN:
                (delighted)
At last, you've come. You'll be taking me to
Helena, then?

                    PIRA:
I beg your pardon...

                   GILLAN:
Helena. You did take your sweet time getting
here, but no matter...

                   TYRAS:
No, Professor. We're moving the entire
library and colony. You'll come with us, of
course.

                   GILLAN:
I've kept her waiting far too long, Tyras.
You know I have. Please, if it isn't too much
trouble...Do you care for olives, Pira?

The professor's odd non sequiturs are hard for
Pira to follow.

                    PIRA:
Not particularly?

                   GILLAN:
What a shame.

                   TYRAS:
Professor, Yanno could use your help with the
pre-Imperial manuscripts. They're so delicate
and must be vacuum sealed before packing.

GILLAN:

Indeed they must. Of course, I shall assist
him at once. Don't leave without me, Pira.
Helena will be so worried.

Gillan departs, humming to himself.

PIRA:

Is he well?

TYRAS:

Not for a very long time, I'm afraid. I'll
have to assign someone to make sure he gets
to the proper transport.

PIRA:

Who is Helena?

TYRAS:

His wife. They were separated during the
relocation. We've tried to find her for years
but no luck.

PIRA:

A familiar story since the supernova. So many
refugees.

TYRAS:

Yes, it is.

Dialogue and music fade as we transition out of
the comm center.

TYRAS (CONT'D):

What if we used the external platforms as
holding areas for the less critical items?

PIRA:

That would be advisable.

INT. *TENDU* - SEVEN/RAFFI'S QUARTERS - DAY

Raffi works her comm panel. Seven pulls on her jacket.

> SEVEN:
> You coming?

> RAFFI:
> Just need a minute to make a quick call.

> SEVEN:
> Shall I get us some coffee?

> RAFFI:
> Only if you want to be my favorite person ever.

> SEVEN:
> And I do.

> RAFFI:
> I'll see you out there.

Seven leaves. Comm channel bleeps open.

> LYSIRA:
> (on comms)
> Raffi? Is that you?

> RAFFI:
> Lieutenant Commander Lysira, as I live and breathe. How's Starfleet's finest analyst doing?

Lysira is Starfleet to the core. (Late 40s.) She and Raffi go way back.

> LYSIRA:
> Really, I'm just surprised that you are, in

fact, still living and breathing. Not to
mention, sober.

RAFFI:
I keep myself out of trouble. Mostly.

LYSIRA:
Not what I'm hearing lately.

RAFFI:
A girl's got to have hobbies.

LYSIRA:
You call facing off with a couple hundred
warbirds to save a few synths using flying
tactical orchids a hobby?

RAFFI:
They were worth saving. But that's not why
I'm calling. I need the down and dirty on a
Romulan warlord named Rynin. Son of former
senator Pomarka.

LYSIRA:
Because?

RAFFI:
Just curious.

LYSIRA:
Raffi...

RAFFI:
I'm thinking about writing a book.

LYSIRA:
This transmission is over.

RAFFI:
Hang on. Wait.

                    LYSIRA:
Raffi, I can't. And you know I can't.

                     RAFFI:
I'm helping a friend, okay? A good friend. A
good friend who's trying to do a noble thing.
And there's a chance I'm going to cross
Rynin's path. Can you help me out here?

Pause.

                    LYSIRA:
No.

                     RAFFI:
Come on.

                    LYSIRA:
Not, no, I can't help you. No, you should
not, under any circumstances, go up against
Rynin without a capitol ship at your back,
and I know you don't have one of those out
there.

                     RAFFI:
He's that bad?

                    LYSIRA:
The most dangerous place to be in the
universe right now is between Rynin and
whatever he wants. He's reckless. And he
doesn't take prisoners.

                     RAFFI:
Come on. That's what they all say.

                    LYSIRA:
We've lost two operatives to him in as many
months.

RAFFI:

Oh.

LYSIRA:

Yeah. Whatever you think you're doing out
there, Raffi, don't. Lysira out.

INT. *TENDU* - BRIDGE - LATER

Pira is speaking over a tinny, static-ridden comm line.

Raffi and Seven join Hyro and Deet talking to Pira.

> HYRO:
> Say again, Pira? Your signal is weak.

> PIRA:
> The defense grid is only at eighty percent of maximum at present.

> DEET:
> [TRANSLATION: That's not going to be sufficient.]

> HYRO:
> You're right, Deet. It won't be sufficient. Not against a warbird.

> SEVEN:
> Have you pulled everything you've got from the backup generators?

> PIRA:
> I believe so.

> SEVEN:
> What about taking power from nonessential systems? You've shut down the library, right?

> PIRA:
> Yes. The entire population is being moved into the caves until the transports arrive.

> RAFFI:
> How far away is Rynin?

PIRA:

Last reported trajectories show him making
orbit in fifty hours.

RAFFI:

How much stuff still needs to be loaded?

PIRA:

All of it.

RAFFI:

(aghast)

Excuse me?

SEVEN:

Pira's ship is just a fighter escort. The
first cargo carriers will be there inside ten
hours—

Professor Gillan's voice interrupts.

GILLAN:

Is that you, Miss Seven?

SEVEN:

Professor Gillan?

GILLAN:

So lovely to hear your voice, dear girl. Have
you come to take me to Helena?

Seven's responses are firm but tender. Her
genuine regard for the professor is clear. For
reasons we don't yet understand, he is dear to
her and her patience with him seems boundless.

SEVEN:

Professor, I need you to clear the line. But
I'll be there in a few hours.

GILLAN:

Helena must be terribly worried about me
right now. The soup will be cold. And the
light will be all wrong.

SEVEN:

I know. Try not to worry. I'll see you very
soon, all right?

GILLAN:

Keep dry. Don't forget your gloves. Do you
still have them?

The comm line fades and dies out with his last words.

SEVEN:

I do.

HYRO:

Comm window's closed. Next one opens in about
two hours.

RAFFI:

I can try to clean up that comm line for you.
Sounds like you're using tin cans and string
for an array.

HYRO:

Unlike those accustomed to a serendipitary
infrastructure...

RAFFI:

That's not even a word.

HYRO:

We're not Starfleet, all right? We use whatever
relays we can find and mountback our signals.

SEVEN:

Piggyback.

                    HYRO:
Pigs have backs?

                    RAFFI:
Yeah, and they're delicious.

                    HYRO:
We can't be talking about the same thing.

                    RAFFI:
We almost never are.

                    SEVEN:
Let it go.

                    RAFFI:
I would, except I just got a little friendly
intel on Rynin, and I'm telling you, anything
you want to save better be off that planet in
the next forty-five hours.

                    HYRO:
Impossible.

                    RAFFI:
Then people are going to die.

                    SEVEN:
Raffi's right.

                    HYRO:
So now we're just meant to take whatever
words fall from her lips as gospel? No,
that's not the word I want.

                    RAFFI:
Actually, it is.

                    SEVEN:
We should change course. Intercept Rynin

before he gets to Ebla. Slow him down. Buy
them more time.

                    RAFFI:
Cool. Great. Except, how many phaser arrays
does this ship have, Hyro?

                    HYRO:
One.

                    RAFFI:
Mmm-hmm. And how many torpedoes?

                    HYRO:
Four.

                    DEET:
[TRANSLATION: Three.]

                    HYRO:
All right, three. I was going to repair the
fourth before we get there.

                    RAFFI:
Doesn't matter. One ship against Rynin is
suicide.

                    SEVEN:
Rynin has no right to Ebla or its people. We
will stop him.

                    RAFFI:
Not with one phaser bank and three torpedoes.

                    HYRO:
Four.

                    RAFFI:
The only way this works, Seven, is if we beat
him there with enough time to evacuate Ebla.

Everything else is a bloodbath. And that's
Starfleet Intelligence talking, not me. How
many ships will we have there in the next
fifteen hours?

                    SEVEN:
Eight, with three carriers.

                    RAFFI:
Will they hold everyone?

                    SEVEN:
If we can take passengers on the *Tendu*.

                    HYRO:
I'll start rearranging the cargo hold.

                    SEVEN:
I'll do it.

                    RAFFI:
I'll give you a hand. Just a second.

Raffi works some magic at Deet's panel.

               RAFFI (CONT'D):
Route all comm signals through these six
bands, and you should be able to at least
hear the people you're talking to.

                    DEET:
[TRANSLATION: Wow. Thanks!]

                    RAFFI:
You're welcome.

INT. *TENDU* - CARGO BAY
CUE: SEVEN AND RAFFI THEME

Seven and Raffi enter the cavernous cargo bay and
take in the untidy space.

> RAFFI:
> No. No, come on, this can't be—

> SEVEN:
> Like you, Hyro doesn't really do clean.

> RAFFI:
> (coughing at the dust)
> Okay, but this is a whole new level of—
> (beat)
> You know what? Doesn't matter. Once we clear
> the dust and crap we could probably get
> forty people in here if they don't mind being
> really close for a while.

Seven quietly gets to work.

> RAFFI (CONT'D):
> So is this you when you're mad?

> SEVEN:
> I'm not mad.

> RAFFI:
> 'Cause I didn't back your play against Rynin?

> SEVEN:
> We wouldn't have to do it alone. We could
> divert a couple of fighters.

> RAFFI:
> Any of 'em bigger than this ship?

> SEVEN:
> No.

RAFFI:
Then when we're all dead, Rynin still gets Ebla.

SEVEN:
That warbird hasn't seen real battle in
years. It's got to have weaknesses. We'll
find them and exploit them.

RAFFI:
I have never in my life met anyone as down-
to-earth as you. Why are you suddenly talking
crazy? You sound just like JL.

SEVEN:
He always seems to manage. And you were more
than willing to follow him anywhere.

RAFFI:
Force of habit. Doesn't mean you don't
learn from your mistakes. We got lucky over
Coppelius.

SEVEN:
And we'll do the same now.

RAFFI:
Look, I don't do magical thinking. Logistics,
targets, tactical analysis, those are my
strong suits.

SEVEN:
            (angry)
It's. Just. Wrong.

RAFFI:
            (gently)
A lot of things are wrong with the universe,
Seven. We try, okay? But not all of them can
be fixed at the end of a phaser rifle.

                    SEVEN:
               (offended)
Is that what you think I'm trying to do here?

                    RAFFI:
I don't know what you have against this guy
Rynin, but you seem very personally invested
in killing him as opposed to saving the
people we're trying to help.

                    SEVEN:
It doesn't have to be personal to be
unacceptable.

                    RAFFI:
Agreed. Look, we're on the same team here and
I just want to make sure our team wins, okay?
We need to prioritize. Cultural artifacts are
important, but not essential. So we focus
on the people. Like that nice man you were
talking to on comms. Get them to safety. Help
them start over. The rest is just stuff.

                    SEVEN:
It's not that simple.

                    RAFFI:
I'm sorry, honey. But right now, it really
is. You said you needed my help. I was
responsible for relocating thousands of
Romulans before the Federation put an end to
our efforts. This is me helping, okay?

                    SEVEN:
It's never enough. I've been trying to make
this part of the galaxy safe for normal
people to just live their damn lives for
decades, and it just never ends.

Seven punctuates that thought by tossing a crate.

> RAFFI:
> I know the feeling.
> (beat)
> Who was that guy, anyway? Professor Gillan?

> SEVEN:
> It's a long story.

> RAFFI:
> We're still hours away from Ebla.

Seven drags something heavy across the deck.

> SEVEN:
> Let's just get this done, okay?

> RAFFI:
> Sure. Okay.

TRANSITION MUSIC: SEVEN AND RAFFI THEME INTO LOVE LETTER THEME

A letter from Gillan to Helena. The first part is read by Gillan, then overlaps briefly as it transitions into Seven's voice.

> GILLAN:
> My dearest Helena, I woke this morning from the most vivid dream. You were in pit twelve on Kemra Prime, dusting off a fragment of second-century fired clay. A vase, if memory serves. So often, these days, it doesn't. The etching looked like a vine...

> SEVEN:
> The etching looked like a vine with those funny six-leaved flowers on it. Do you remember? The blue hadn't faded. You looked

up at me, wiping ancient dust across your cheek and smiling like you'd unwrapped a present the hill people had hidden just for you, nine thousand years ago. "I found it," you cried out. "It is blue. I told you it would be." Why haven't I heard from you, my love? I must know you are safe. Please, as soon as you get this, just a line or two. I shall sleep better. Until then, I will always find you in my dreams. Always...

CUE: LOVE LETTER THEME FADES

INT. *TENDU* **- BRIDGE**
CUE: DEET'S MUSICAL SELECTION SOFT
IN THE BACKGROUND - UPBEAT LATIN

Seven, Raffi, Hyro, and Deet on the bridge. Pira
and Tyras on comms.

                    TYRAS:
                (over comms)
     Ebla Ground confirms load Seventeen Bravo is
     on the transporter pad.

                    HYRO:
     The carrier *Sublime* has coordinates locked.
     Initiate transport.

                    DEET:
     [TRANSLATION: Transport complete.]

                    RAFFI:
     Okay, Deet. That's nine percent of Ebla's
     cargo loaded. The carrier *Sublime* can take
     two more loads but that's it.

                    DEET:
     [TRANSLATION: We still have a long way to go.]

                    RAFFI:
     Yes, yes, we do have a ways to go yet. But
     we'll get there, right? Hyro, where are the
     other three ships you promised me?

                    HYRO:
     Three? Did I say three?

                    RAFFI:
     Us, Pira's ship, three carriers—of which we
     have two right now, *Sublime* and *Chrysalis*—and
     three more for defense.

                         HYRO:
The others are on their way, I assume.
There's still plenty of time.

                         RAFFI:
On whose clock?

                         PIRA:
                    (over comms)
Pira to Seven: Can you divert your long-range
sensors to grid nine six two mark four. I'm
picking up an unusual distortion.

                         SEVEN:
On it.

As Seven checks her sensors, Tyras comes again
over comms.

                         TYRAS:
The first group of personnel are on pad three.
They'll be coming up in groups of five.

                         RAFFI:
Carrier *Chrysalis* is standing by. How many in
this group again?

                         TYRAS:
Twenty-five.

                         RAFFI:
Copy that. Send 'em up.

                         HYRO:
Despite your negative ninny-ness, I think
things are going quite well, so far.

                         SEVEN:
Raffi, take a look at this sensor feed for me.

                    RAFFI:
You just had to say it, didn't you, Hyro?
          (to Seven)
What is it?

                    SEVEN:
It could be a sensor anomaly. But I don't
like it.

                    RAFFI:
Rynin is still thirty hours out, right?

                    SEVEN:
According to our tracking.

                    RAFFI:
And how good is your tracking?

                    SEVEN:
The *Forever Free* missed its last two checks,
but there was an ion storm in their path.
They had to alter course.

                    RAFFI:
Can we detect tachyon emissions at this
distance?

                    SEVEN:
Can now.
          (beat)
Oh. That's a lot of tachyons.

                    RAFFI:
Yeah, could be a glitch. But it's probably...

                    SEVEN:
A cloaked warbird. Rynin's early.

                    RAFFI:
Mmm-hmm.

Seven shouts over the low-level comm chatter and music.

                    SEVEN:
    Hyro, we're about to have company.

                    HYRO:
    Friend or foe?

                    RAFFI:
    Rynin.

                    HYRO:
    Understood. Deet, clear the comm lines and cut the music.

Music ends sharply.

                    DEET:
    [TRANSLATION: Go ahead.]

                    HYRO:
    This is the *Tendu* to all Ranger ships. Cease transports. Raise shields. Carriers, prepare to break orbit and go to warp. Set course for rendezvous point. Tyras, as soon as they're clear, bring up the planetary defense grid. Pira, look sharp. You and I are about to engage Rynin's warbird.
            (beat)
    Deet, raise *Tendu*'s shields and bring phasers and torpedoes online.

                    DEET:
    [TRANSLATION: Understood.]

                    HYRO:
    Thank you, Deet.

SEVEN:
We need to cover the carriers until they can
go to warp.

RAFFI:
That still leaves a lot of unprotected people
on the surface.

SEVEN:
One problem at a time.

RAFFI:
First target is his shield emitters, right,
Hyro?

HYRO:
First target is anything we can hit.

RAFFI:
Your resources are limited. Don't waste them.

HYRO:
Did I miss a meeting? I don't actually work
for you, do I?

SEVEN:
Hyro. Raffi. Rynin is the enemy here.

Suddenly the ship is hit by a phaser blast.

HYRO:
And there he is. Oh, lovely. He's christmased
his ship the *Wrath*.

SEVEN:
Christened.

RAFFI:
At least we know Rynin doesn't do subtlety.

                    HYRO:
Look sharp, Deet. We don't want to take too
many of those disruptor cannon hits.

CUE: SPACE BATTLE MUSIC

Multiple phaser arrays firing. Explosion on *Tendu*
bridge.

                    SEVEN:
Our shields are at thirty-three percent. We
can take one more hit, maybe two.

                    RAFFI:
And we're out of torpedoes.

                    HYRO:
Chrysalis is away. The *Sublime* is almost
clear. Keep that warbird off her tail, Deet.

                    DEET:
  [TRANSLATION: Doing my best.]

                    HYRO:
I know you are.

Another boom.

                    RAFFI:
The *Wrath* is coming around. Targeting Pira's
ship.

                    SEVEN:
Pira, Rynin's on your tail.

                    PIRA:
            (over comms)
I am aware.

                    RAFFI:
He's got a target lock.

PIRA:
(over comms)
Port thruster isn't responding. *Tendu*, can
you...

Pira's comm line cuts abruptly, followed by a
loud boom as Pira's ship is destroyed.

RAFFI:
That son of a bitch.

HYRO:
At least both carriers were able to go to
warp. They're safe. And Pira gave her life
for them.

RAFFI:
Leaving us as Rynin's only target.

HYRO:
For all things there is a seasoning. Deet, come
back around and run straight at the *Wrath*.

RAFFI:
A frontal assault?

HYRO:
And avoid getting hit, obviously.

DEET:
(the word "remora" is clearly heard)
[TRANSLATION: Are we going to remora?]

HYRO:
Yes, Deet, we're going to remora.

RAFFI:
What's remora?

Another small boom along with incoming Romulan
phaser fire and small shield impacts.

HYRO:
It's really quite simple, Miss Raffaela.
Assuming we survive the run, we get right
under her belly and match her course and
speed.

SEVEN:
Disappearing from her sensors.

RAFFI:
Won't take long for them to figure out where
we are.

DEET:
[TRANSLATION: Hang on, everyone!]

Loud screech of metal as Deet pulls a hard turn.

Suddenly everything gets quiet.

HYRO:
Deet, match course and speed.

DEET:
[TRANSLATION: Done.]

HYRO:
Excellent job, Deet.

A pause as everyone catches their breath.

HYRO (CONT'D):
Any chance Rynin is altering course to follow
the carriers?

RAFFI:
Doesn't look like it. He's heading straight
for the planetary defense grid.

HYRO:
Why? Why give up the cargo he came to steal?

SEVEN:

Maybe because he scanned the holds and realized they were mostly empty?

Heavy static on the comms as they crackle to life.

TYRAS:
(over comms)
This is Tyras to any Fenris ship still in range. The defense grid is falling. Repeat, the defense—

Before she can finish, the sound of a massive explosion in the distance is heard over the line just before it goes dead.

RAFFI:

Get them back, Deet.

DEET:

[TRANSLATION: Working on it.]

RAFFI:

Tell them not to resist. Just run and hide. Let Rynin have whatever he wants.

HYRO:

Agreed. That last hit took the planet's defense grid below twenty percent.

SEVEN:

A shuttle is launching from the *Wrath*. It's heading for the surface.

RAFFI:

Heavily armed?

SEVEN:

No, actually. Minimal weapons. Ten life signs.

                    RAFFI:
Any transporter activity? Maybe he's just going
to try to grab whatever he can get from orbit.

                    SEVEN:
None.

                    HYRO:
He's going to slaughter them. Listen to them
scream. Watch them beg for their lives,
shoveling before him.

                    RAFFI:
Groveling.
          (beat)
Jeez, now you've got me doing it.

                    HYRO:
          (continuing)
And then he's going to take his sweet time
collecting the spoils.

                    DEET:
[TRANSLATION: What an asshole.]

                    RAFFI:
Yes, Deet, he is definitely an asshole. But
that's not really Rynin's style, is it?

                    SEVEN:
Unless he's after something specific.

                    RAFFI:
Any idea what?

                    SEVEN:
No. We have to get down there.

                    HYRO:
And do what?

SEVEN:

At the very least, find out what's so damned important to him.

HYRO:

The defense grid has fallen.

SEVEN:

What do you say, Raffi? You up for a little close-contact assault?

RAFFI:

Honest answer?

SEVEN:

Only if it's yes.

RAFFI:

Just give me a damn phaser rifle. And Deet, keep a lock on our signals at all times.

DEET:

[TRANSLATION: Understood.]

EXT. EBLA SURFACE - DAY
SOUND OF FENRIS RANGER TRANSPORTER

Distant shouting, children crying. A disruptor
fires and someone screams in terror.

>   CENTURIAN:
>   (shouts over the crowd)
>   Where is he?

Seven and Raffi converse in tense whispers.

>   SEVEN:
>   Come on. We have to help them.

>   RAFFI:
>   Hold up.

Raffi drags Seven behind cover.

>   SEVEN:
>   Raffi, the fight's that way.

>   RAFFI:
>   Look at it. No one is fighting. You've got
>   about forty people lined up along the side of
>   the building.

>   SEVEN:
>   With Romulan disruptors pointed at them.

>   RAFFI:
>   I was told to expect a bloodbath. This isn't it.

>   SEVEN:
>   Yet. This isn't it yet. We can still stop them.

>   RAFFI:
>   Fine. What's your plan?

>   SEVEN:
>   This, for a start.

Seven steps out of cover and fires four distinct shots. Sound of four bodies falling to the ground as crowd screams/shouts/cries in fear.

                    SEVEN (CONT'D):
Four Romulans down.

                    RAFFI:
A little warning before you start shooting next time? What if you'd missed?

                    SEVEN:
I don't miss.

Seven breaks cover and addresses the crowd.

                    SEVEN (CONT'D):
Back to the caves! Run.

Confused shouts and scuffling as the crowd starts to disperse.

                    RAFFI:
Seven, look over there. By the Romulan shuttle.

                    SEVEN:
That's Professor Gillan.

                    RAFFI:
How old is he? And why are six guys guarding him? The hell sense does that make?

                    SEVEN:
Cover me. I'm going after him.

                    RAFFI:
Not right now, you're not.

                    SEVEN:
It's six guys. They're not even looking at us. And they're ignoring the colonists.

                    RAFFI:
And the guys you just shot. Because they
are clearly under orders to get that man to
Rynin. Why? What's so important about him?

                    SEVEN:
I don't know. I just know what Rynin will do
to him, and I'm not going to let that happen.

Seven takes off toward the transport.

                    RAFFI:
          (loud but not too loud)
Wait! Wait! Shit!
          (she thinks fast)
Raffi to *Tendu*. Hyro?

                    HYRO:
          (on comms)
Go ahead.

                    RAFFI:
Lock onto Seven this second and transport her
back to the ship.

                    HYRO:
She's in motion.

                    RAFFI:
Now, Hyro!

Exchange of phaser/disruptor fire. Then a Fenris
Ranger transporter in the distance.

Roar of engines powering up as the Romulan
shuttle lifts off the surface of Ebla.

                RAFFI (CONT'D):
Did you get her, Hyro? Hyro!?!!

ACT TWO

INT. *WRATH* - BRIDGE

CUE: ROMULANS SING A TRADITIONAL SONG OF VICTORY

Rynin enters and addresses his second-in-command, Koliva.

> KOLIVA:
> *Emperor on the bridge!*

> RYNIN:
> Well done, servants of the new empire.

A hearty cheer erupts.

> RYNIN (CONT'D):
> Our prize has been claimed. Our victory is
> now assured.

Another cheer.

> RYNIN (CONT'D):
> Report, Koliva.

> KOLIVA:
> Sensors show no sign that we are being followed.
> We never regained contact with the Ranger ship.
> It must have fled, just as you said it would.

> RYNIN:
> They fear us now. But soon, they will bow
> before us and the empire we are building.

> KOLIVA:
> To the empire!

> CREW:
> To the empire!

> KOLIVA:
> What is our new course, Emperor?

> RYNIN:
> Eternity, Koliva. We are headed for eternity.

INT. *TENDU* **- SEVEN/RAFFI'S QUARTERS - DAY**

> RAFFI:
>
> Oh, thank God, you made it. What were you thinking? You don't take on six guys alone.

> SEVEN:
> (cold)
>
> I was a drone for eighteen years. Incapable of individual thought or agency. My thoughts are now my own. As are my choices. Got it?

> RAFFI:
>
> I do.

INT. *WRATH* **- HOLDING CELL**

Rynin's guard roughly pushes Gillan along.

> GILLAN:
> You needn't push, my good man. I am every bit
> as anxious to reach Helena as—

> GUARD:
> Quiet!

The footsteps stop, and we hear the electric hum
of a cell force field.

> GUARD (CONT'D):
> Into the cell.

The hum deactivates.

> GILLAN:
> Are you quite certain...?

> GUARD:
> GET IN!

We hear a brief scuffle as the guard pushes
Gillan into the cell. Gillan hits the cell floor.

> GILLAN:
> Oh!

> GUARD:
> Don't bother trying to escape. No one—

A sudden blast of disruptor fire. The guard
screams as he disintegrates.

> GILLAN:
> (stunned horror)
> Where did he... Is he...?

RYNIN:
I told him to treat you well. He failed to
do so and paid with his life, as do all who
disobey my orders.
(beat)
You are our honored guest, Professor. I am
Emperor Rynin, and I am at your service.

GILLAN:
Rynin...Yes, thank you, sir. I knew someone
would be coming along soon, and I cannot
thank you enough for taking me to Helena. How
long until we arrive?

RYNIN:
That depends on you, my friend.

GILLAN:
The tomatillos will be at the peak of ripeness.
There will be tea, of course, in the blue
pitcher. Have you ever had a Roskan tomato?

RYNIN:
No. Delicious, I'm sure. But of course, you
did not expect me to go so far out of my way
for free. In exchange for your safe passage,
I require the Lemniscate.

GILLAN:
The...Lemniscate?

RYNIN:
I first read the tale of the Lemniscate in
my great-grandfather's writings. The token of
eternity that grants eternal life. Of course,
he meant to scare his readers. The story was
a warning. "The most miserable man alive is
he who cannot die."

Rynin laughs.

>   RYNIN (CONT'D):
> Can you imagine? Fearing something so
> magnificent?

>   GILLAN:
> No, but...

CUE: RYNIN'S THEME

>   RYNIN:
> No, you cannot. Because like me, you
> understand its worth. Its power. Its purpose.
>   (beat)
> Do you remember him? Tralyn, son of Grevis?

>   GILLAN:
> I've met so many good and decent Romulans.
> I'm sure he was one of them.

>   RYNIN:
> Tralyn despised weakness. A lesson passed
> down from father to son. My father, too,
> learned to despise himself. My blood is
> tainted, you see. So Pomarka abandoned me and
> my mother. Cast us out. I spent many years
> seeking the family he denied me. All they had
> is now mine. Including this image.

>   GILLAN:
> Oh, yes. Cavalas Prime. That was long before
> I met Helena, though.

>   RYNIN:
> This image was captured two centuries ago.
> You and my great-grandfather. The Lemniscate
> is no legend. It is real. Otherwise, you,

too, would be long dead. And you don't look
particularly miserable.

                    GILLAN:
No, you're not listening. The light on
Helena's face was just...I went to fill the
kettle, and—

                    RYNIN:
Professor.

                    GILLAN:
—and if I'm not there, the, the tomatillo
soup will be cold. The soup is—

                    RYNIN:
          (shouts)
Professor!!
          (calmly)
The sooner I have what I need, the sooner
you will be with Helena again, sipping warm
tomatillo soup. Just tell me. Where is the
Lemniscate?

                    GILLAN:
It's with Helena, of course!

                    RYNIN:
          (barely contained fury)
And. Where. Is. Helena?

                    GILLAN:
She's where you're taking me! She's home!
Waiting for me.

                    RYNIN:
Where is home?!!

GILLAN:

It's...wherever Helena is.

RYNIN:

(small sigh)

Not miserable then. But mad.

(beat)

Rest now, Professor. We'll talk again soon.

INT. EBLA COMM CENTER - EVENING

Hyro and Tyras are planning their next move.
Raffi enters.

                    RAFFI:
    Where's Seven?

                    HYRO:
    I believe her exact words were—

                    RAFFI:
    Never mind. She's obviously still mad at me.
    She'll get over it.

                    HYRO:
    Tyras, this is Miss Raffaela. She's new.

                    TYRAS:
    Thank you for your service.

                    RAFFI:
    Not a problem. I just wish we could have done
    more.

                    HYRO:
    Rynin ignored the *Tendu*. Jumped straight to
    warp. The two carriers have been recalled.
    They'll make orbit within five hours, and the
    evacuation will continue.

                    TYRAS:
    If we could restore the defense grid and bring
    it to full power, it might not be necessary.

                    RAFFI:
    I'm sorry, Tyras, is it?

                    TYRAS:
    Chief Archivist, yes.

RAFFI:

Your best defense was never a twenty-year-
old, hastily-cobbled-together planetary
shield. It was the fact that no one knew you
were here. Even if Rynin doesn't come back,
others will. You have to get out, now, while
you still can.

TYRAS:

Hyro?

HYRO:
(kindly)
In this, and only in this, Miss Raffaela and
I are in agreement.

RAFFI:

Can you tell me anything about the man they
took?

TYRAS:

Professor Gillan?

RAFFI:

Why would a Romulan warlord be so interested
in him?

TYRAS:

I can't imagine. Gillan is brilliant. His
memory can be extraordinary and incredibly
detailed. You'd swear when he was talking
about the ruins at Havra that he'd walked
their streets a thousand years ago. He and
his wife excavated dozens of critical sites,
or they did, before the supernova.

RAFFI:

His wife?

TYRAS:

Helena. He was found alone on Gorvan and
ended up in some refugee camp. The Rangers
brought him here but never found any trace of
her. We were thrilled to have him. But when
he's having an off day, he can be difficult
to manage.

RAFFI:

Off?

TYRAS:

Every ship that comes here he thinks is
meant to transport him back to her. I
tried to hide him from Rynin's men, but he
went willingly. Almost like a child. He
thought...

Tyras is overwhelmed by emotion at the memory.

HYRO:

You did all you could, friend. His madness
might have saved his life. Imagine if he had
resisted.

RAFFI:

Not to mention the lives of everyone else in
the colony.

TYRAS:

Still, if I'd done more, perhaps...

RAFFI:

Are there any records here on him, any work
he's done, I could take a look at?

HYRO:

Why?

RAFFI:

Because Rynin took him for a reason, and I
haven't heard a good one yet.

TYRAS:

Everything the professor worked on was in our
library database. I'll grant you access from
your ship.

RAFFI:

Perfect. Thanks.

HYRO:

Seven wants to go after him, you know. She
was furious with me as well.

RAFFI:

I apologize for saving her life. You happy now?

HYRO:

Over the lagoon.

Raffi laughs.

RAFFI:

Over the moon, Hyro.

HYRO:

That makes no sense. It's not as if moons
have a top or a bottom. How can one be over a
moon?

RAFFI:

Doesn't matter. She'll come around, right?

HYRO:

Honestly, I've never seen her like this.
Most of the time she's so calm. Detached.
Professional. Now she's like a raw nerve. Do
I have you to thank for that as well?

                    RAFFI:
I'll talk to her.

                    HYRO:
Or, maybe think about just giving her a
little space. You can't force your way past
her defenses. They're too well fortified.

                    RAFFI:
You know her pretty well, huh?

                    HYRO:
As well as she'll allow.

                    RAFFI:
Fine. I'll give her some space. Do the
research. Just make sure she doesn't do
anything stupid, okay?

**CUE: TRANSITION AS LOVE LETTER THEME FADES UP.
ANOTHER LETTER, READ IN SEVEN'S VOICE.**

                    SEVEN:
Good morning, my love. The olives here are
terrible. My fellow refugees actually prefer
them straight from the trees. Ghastly. Salt
is in short supply, or I'd introduce them to
your lovely brine. Of course, nothing can be
right when you aren't here. I keep wondering
what I could have done differently. So many
things, I suppose. I should never have waited
so long to tell you how I felt. I thought
I'd seen all life had to offer. That you
would quickly move on and forget me. Can you
forgive me for being so foolish? For wasting
so many days we could have shared? I'd trade
all of them for one more moment with you. I
must find us some salt. More soon.

INT. *TENDU* **- RAFFI'S QUARTERS**

Cue: emo grunge piece Deet is listening to on the *Tendu*. The music is muted through the closed door. The sound of Raffi furiously tapping keys on her computer interface.

> RAFFI:
>> Come on, come on.

When it finally "speaks," it is in the gruff, impatient voice of a Klingon.

> INTERFACE:
>> *QAPLA'!*

> RAFFI:
>> Hello?

> INTERFACE:
>> *BE'BATLH DAGHAJ'A?*

> RAFFI:
>> (shouting)
>> DEET!?

Brief pause. Door opens.

> DEET:
>> (in perfect English)
>> You bellowed?

> RAFFI:
>> Why is this thing yelling at me in Klingon? Wait. Why are you speaking Federation Standard?

> DEET:
>> It's Hyro's ship. I won't insult his beliefs. But I've always found translators very useful.

                RAFFI:

I like you so much.

                DEET:

And I, you, Miss Raffaela.

                RAFFI:

Can you fix this thing?

                DEET:

The only functioning index appears to be
Klingon. Let me see if I can...

Then, same voice, same Klingon intensity, but in
English.

                INTERFACE:

GREETINGS. HOW MAY I ASSIST YOU?

                DEET:

Better?

                RAFFI:

It'll do.

                DEET:

You won't tell Hyro, will you?

                RAFFI:

Tell Hyro what? Nothin' to tell here. Thanks,
Deet.

                INTERFACE:

I AWAIT YOUR QUERY!

Sound of door opening and closing again.

                RAFFI:

Show me everything you have on Professor
Gillan.

INTERFACE:

WORKING!

RAFFI:

Okay. So you came to Ebla in '87. Made notes
in sixty-two hundred articles—so you were
busy. Let's see—*Mystic Rites of the Batibeh
Clans*...*Gnostilak: A Requiem*—interesting but
not really helpful. Interface?

INTERFACE:

DO YOU HAVE A QUERY?

RAFFI:

I do. And stop shouting. Show me images of
Gillan.
    (beat)
Wow. How did you age fifty years in the last
five? Poor guy. What species is Gillan?

INTERFACE:

UNKNOWN.

RAFFI:

Are there any records of his activities or
articles prior to his arrival at Ebla?
    (beat)
Whoa. Somebody really got around. 2385, six
different archeological sites; 2381—hang
on—2219? That has to be a mistake. I mean, it
looks like him, but the year...

INTERFACE:

I DO NOT MAKE MISTAKES!

RAFFI:

Oh, calm down. Interface, I'm going to cross-
link your archive to my personal Starfleet

database, and I want you to search for any
other images of Gillan prior to 2219.

                    INTERFACE:
WORKING!

                    RAFFI:
And while you're doing that, I'm going to
make a note that Tyras needs to work on your
people skills.
          (beat)
2172. 2119. 2073? Interface, what is the
oldest known image of this man?

                    INTERFACE:
SHANTIGA VI, BALARA SECTOR, LOCAL CALENDAR
15932, YEAR OF THE GANHAK!

                    RAFFI:
What does that translate to by Starfleet
reckoning?

                    INTERFACE:
GREGORIAN 879.

                    RAFFI:
Excuse me?

                    INTERFACE:
YOU ARE EXCUSED!

Transition as grunge music fades, replaced by
Seven and Raffi theme.

EXT. EBLA - SHIP GRAVEYARD, NIGHT

Raffi approaches Seven, who is elbow deep in the
innards of a small, grounded shuttle.

> RAFFI:
> Nothing like a little Class-J shuttle repair
> to take your mind off your troubles, amirite?

> SEVEN:
> Go away.

Whir of a pneumatic drill starting up.

> RAFFI:
> I'm sorry, okay? But in fairness, I did tell
> you I'm not Ranger material. The stunts you
> guys pull, Starfleet would never...

> SEVEN:
> I left Starfleet for a reason, you know?

> RAFFI:
> Fair point.
> (beat)
> I come bearing gifts.

> SEVEN:
> What gifts?

> RAFFI:
> Information. And some Romulan ale—at least I
> think that's what it is. I found it in Hyro's
> cargo hold. Deet swears by it.

Sound of Seven taking a swig and spitting it out.

> SEVEN:
> Ugh.

                    RAFFI:
I've had worse.
          (gently)
I bet you have too.

                    SEVEN:
It tastes like deck solvent.

                    RAFFI:
So this is your plan? You're gonna get this
thing space-worthy and go after the professor
all by your lonesome?

                    SEVEN:
If I have to.

                    RAFFI:
How well do you know the professor?

                    SEVEN:
I found him in a refugee camp on Stalvi. You
know what they were like...the first Romulan
resettlements? Tents and filth and guards who
didn't care that these were their own people
suffering.

                    RAFFI:
But what drew you to him? There had to be
thousands of people in that camp.

Transition to sounds of Romulan refugee camp:
pouring rain, footsteps sloshing through mud,
the hum of an electric fence, people chattering,
guards shouting in the distance, children crying,
and finally the welcoming crackle of a warm fire.

EXT. REFUGEE CAMP, NIGHT (FLASHBACK)

Footsteps approach the fire as Gillan's voice,
distraught, fades up along with the rustling of papers.

> GILLAN:
> No, no, that's not it! Where is it?
> (addressing Seven directly)
> Have you seen it? It's here somewhere.

> SEVEN:
> I'm sorry—what are you looking for?

> GILLAN:
> The light. It was early morning. Solaris was
> rising. She was asleep.
> (beat)
> The light moved across her face so slowly.
> Her eyes were closed but the lashes caught the
> beam—I so loved watching her sleep—it was a
> secret, our secret, a million precious moments
> that were our treasures. I didn't get the
> chance to tell her, and she will want to know.

> SEVEN:
> Sir, please calm down.

> GILLAN:
> Look here. Take these. I'll look through the
> others. It was only yesterday, I, I had it in
> my hands.

> SEVEN:
> These are—letters?

> GILLAN:
> (reading)
> "...remember when I told you about the
> Retuans? Their special fondness for shells?

And we traced their symbol for unity on that
white stone?"
            (back to Seven)
No, that's not it either. But that was a
perfect day. Have you ever had one of those?

                SEVEN:
Not that I can recall.

                GILLAN:
Your hands, dear. They're like ice.

                SEVEN:
I'm fine.

                GILLAN:
No, come warm them by the fire. Your glove
is barely whole. That won't do. Wait, I have
just the thing.
            (beat)
Here. These gloves were Helena's. She won't
mind. Your hands are smaller, but no matter.

                SEVEN:
They're lovely. But I couldn't possibly...

                GILLAN:
Those gloves have touched the dirt of
hundreds of worlds. When you find her, you
can return them to her.

                SEVEN:
Where is she?

                GILLAN:
We were separated. Kind people. Huge white ship.
But they didn't understand. They forced me to
go. I didn't want to. I've lost her, you see.

Gillan begins to weep at the memory.

SEVEN:

I'm sorry. The evacuations are happening so quickly. Many people have been separated from their loved ones. But this is only temporary.

GILLAN:

I can't live without her.

SEVEN:

Sir...

GILLAN:

Gillan. Professor of antiquities.

SEVEN:

Gillan, I'm Seven.

GILLAN:

What a beautiful name. Were you on the white ship?

SEVEN:

No. I'm a Fenris Ranger. We're helping the refugees.

GILLAN:

That's me now, isn't it?

Sound of rustling papers.

GILLAN (CONT'D):

You must find her. You must find Helena. Take these letters. She'll want to know where I've been and what I've been thinking. Every detail mattered to her. The smallest color, the purest line. Please, take them and tell her where I am. She'll come for me. I know it.

Sounds of the refugee camp fade as we transition back to the surface of Ebla.

EXT. EBLA - SHIP GRAVEYARD, NIGHT

Raffi and Seven as before. Seven still tinkering
with the ship's engine.

> RAFFI:
>
> Did you ever find her?

> SEVEN:
>
> Not yet. Records had her entering the Gorvan
> system, which was one of the last evacuated
> worlds. When I learned that Gillan was the
> most revered historian in the quadrant, I went
> back to Stalvi. Brought him here. And kept
> looking for her, any chance I got. Still am.

> RAFFI:
>
> Did you know he is over two thousand years old?

> SEVEN:
>
> No. What?

> RAFFI:
>
> I'm not sure what the Rangers' databases are
> like, but Starfleet has records on this man
> that go back to the ninth century.

> SEVEN:
>
> I thought he was human.

> RAFFI:
>
> Unlikely. He probably was the most valuable
> thing on this planet. There's no telling what
> Rynin wanted with him, but I guarantee it
> wasn't just to kill him. If you really want to
> do this, let's make a plan and do it right.

> SEVEN:
>
> Stand back.

Both of them stand clear. Then, just as the
engine hum starts to stabilize, a harsh rattle is
followed by a small explosion.

> SEVEN (CONT'D):
> Damn it.

> RAFFI:
> I love the fact that you don't know how to
> quit, Seven. But this one is a goner.

> SEVEN:
> I'll find another one.

> RAFFI:
> What is this place? It's like an elephant
> graveyard, but for ships.

> SEVEN:
> Sometimes the Rangers find abandoned ships
> out there and tow them to safe planets.
> Mostly for parts.

> RAFFI:
> You guys really are holding this part of the
> galaxy together with your bare hands, aren't
> you?

> SEVEN:
> I can't just let him go.

> RAFFI:
> He really got in under the radar, didn't he?

> SEVEN:
> I don't know what you mean.

> RAFFI:
> I mean, in the kindest and most loving way
> possible, you keep people at a distance. On

purpose. How did this professor who you can't have known for more than a few days get past those formidable defenses?

                    SEVEN:
His letters, I suppose.

CUE: LOVE LETTER THEME

                    SEVEN (CONT'D):
The ones he gave me for Helena. I've read them a thousand times. I've never known a mind, a man, quite like him. He'll go on and on about the smallest detail of a moment they shared, things most people would never bother to remember. But more than that, he adores her in a way I didn't know was possible. I've never felt anything like what he does for Helena.

                    RAFFI:
True love, huh?

                    SEVEN:
He almost let her go when they first met. She wanted more and he wasn't having it. But one day, he just surrendered. Made her the center of his universe. And to hear him tell it, every moment after that was filled with wonder and joy and purpose and all the things life is supposed to be about. Can you imagine losing that?

                    RAFFI:
I can't imagine having it.

                    SEVEN:
No?

                    RAFFI:
Good times. Fun. Great sex. All of that, I've
had. And then some. But somehow, I've never
been enough for anyone.

                    SEVEN:
Neither have I.

                    RAFFI:
Something else we have in common.
          (beat)
Come sit down.

Seven sits next to Raffi on the ground.

                    SEVEN:
          (weary)
I'm still mad at you.

                    RAFFI:
It's okay. I can take it.
          (beat)
Do you remember when you first transported
aboard *La Sirena*?

                    SEVEN:
Not really. Didn't I pass out?

                    RAFFI:
What you missed was my heart stopping in my
chest the very first time I saw you.

                    SEVEN:
You covered it pretty well.

                    RAFFI:
I'm good at that. I'm great at that. I didn't
come out here for Ebla or the Rangers. I came
for you.

                          SEVEN:
I know.

                          RAFFI:
So don't push me away. You're safe here. I
promise. You don't have to solve all of the
universe's problems alone.

                          SEVEN:
You're not the first person to tell me that.

                          RAFFI:
I don't want to be the first. I just want to
be the last.

                          SEVEN:
                   (deeply touched)
Where the hell did you come from?

                          RAFFI:
Let's get back to the ship.

                          SEVEN:
Not yet. Stay here with me. Under the stars.

They kiss.

INT. *WRATH* - BRIDGE
CUE: RYNIN'S THEME

Rynin approaches Koliva, who taps at her console.

RYNIN:
Koliva, report!

KOLIVA:
I've searched all available records for the
location where the professor and his wife
lived the longest.

RYNIN:
And?

KOLIVA:
(nervous)
There isn't one, my Emperor. Fifty years
ago the professor and his wife were granted
permission by the Romulan Cultural Ministry
to research and excavate ancient Imperial
sites.

RYNIN:
Why would the Ministry allow a pair of non-
Romulans such freedom of movement within the
Empire?

KOLIVA:
His reputation, I assume. They never stayed
in one place for long. Certainly not long
enough for any of the places to be called
their "home."

A crewman approaches.

CREWMAN:
Your meal, my Emperor—

Rynin smacks the meal tray out of the crewman's hands. The soup splashes onto Rynin's clothes.

                    RYNIN:
    Not now!

                    CREWMAN:
    I'm sorry, sir, I'll clean it up—

                    RYNIN:
    Fool. Now I'm wearing my meal. It looks like
    a human bled to death on me.
                (beat, thinking)
    Red...
                (beat)
    Koliva, search for a world named Roska.

                    KOLIVA:
    Sir?

                    RYNIN:
    Do it, Koliva. Eternity is waiting.

Koliva works her console.

                    KOLIVA:
    I have something. Roska. In the Napiri
    Sector. No known settlements.

                    RYNIN:
    Set course at once.

EXT. EBLA SHIP GRAVEYARD - MORNING

Raffi wakes alone, stands up.

> RAFFI:
> (her head is pounding)
> Ugh. Deet, Deet, what did you do to me.
> (big yawn and stretch)
> Seven? Seven?

Raffi searches for Seven. Chirp as Raffi
activates her comms.

> RAFFI (CONT'D):
> Raffi to Hyro. You there?

> HYRO:
> (loud over comms)
> Good morning.

> RAFFI:
> For the love, Hyro, take the volume down a
> little.

Hyro does not.

> HYRO:
> Lovely day ahead. No sign of interluders.

> RAFFI:
> Where's Seven? Is she on the *Tendu*?

> HYRO:
> No. She left hours ago. Didn't she tell you?
> Taza loaned her one of his small tactical
> flyers.

> RAFFI:
> (now wide-awake)
> She left? You let her go after Rynin alone?

                    HYRO:
She's a Ranger. Not my eight-year-old niece.

                    RAFFI:
Don't Rangers look out for one another?
Realize when someone is making a terrible
mistake? Do you care about each other at all?

                    HYRO:
Rangers are devoted but flexible. On the
whole, we function best in the absence of
boundaries. Just like Starfleet, but the
opposite.

                    RAFFI:
I want you to know, Hyro, that the next time
I see you, I am going to murder you with my
bare hands.

                    HYRO:
Not a morning person, are we? Good to know.
Tendu out.

                    RAFFI:
Hyro, don't you dare...
          (but he has cut the line)
Hyro!!

Footsteps approaching.

                    DEET:
    Raffi.

                    RAFFI:
Deet. Were you there when Seven left?

                    DEET:
Seven left?

RAFFI:

I can't believe it. I thought we were—I
poured out my damn soul to her and she just—

DEET:

Perhaps that was your mistake.

RAFFI:

Beg pardon?

DEET:

Humans are dumb when they are afraid.

RAFFI:

What is she afraid of? Never mind. I thought
we were on the same page, but clearly, I was
wrong. I have to get off this planet.

DEET:

Then you will want to see what I came to
show you.

RAFFI:

What?

DEET:

Come with me.

EXT. ROSKA - MORNING
CUE: PROFESSOR'S THEME

Hum of a Romulan transporter as Rynin and Gillan beam down to the surface of Roska.

> GILLAN:
> (listens to birdsong)
> The flittits are here early this season!

> RYNIN:
> This is it, isn't it? Roska. This cabin. Your home.

> GILLAN:
> (confused)
> Wait. Those are lilac warblers. Yes, that would explain the change in migration—

> RYNIN:
> Professor. Open the door.

> GILLAN:
> I've lost the key.

A crash as Rynin kicks the door off its hinges.

> RYNIN:
> Don't need one.

Rynin and Gillan enter and move through the room.

> RYNIN (CONT'D):
> Now, where is the Lemniscate?

> GILLAN:
> I told you, the Lemniscate is with Helena. At home.

> RYNIN:
> This is your home!

Rynin starts trashing the room.

GILLAN:
Please, no. You mustn't. Helena will—

More sounds of Rynin trashing the room. Rynin
finally stops, exhaling from the exertion.

CUE: RYNIN'S THEME

RYNIN:
Don't lie to me. Helena's not here. She
would never come back here. You were
separated just before Romulus was destroyed,
but you gave her the Lemniscate first. You
protected her—and it—by telling everyone
she was lost. You've waited all this time
for her to come to you, to finally be
reunited. But she's not here. She's never
coming home.

GILLAN:
(upset)
Home is wherever Helena is.

RYNIN:
You gave her the gift of eternal life. Why
would she waste that on you?

GILLAN:
(tearful, distraught)
Stop it! You don't understand—

RYNIN:
She never loved an old fool like you. She
only wanted what you could give her. And
when you gave her the Lemniscate, she left
you behind, didn't she? Where would she
have gone?

GILLAN:
(tearful)
The light...

RYNIN:
Where is she?

GILLAN:
(softly)
The shaft of light...do you see it there, how it falls?

CUE: PROFESSOR'S THEME TRANSITION TO LOVE LETTER THEME

Seven reads.

SEVEN:
My darling, please forgive me. I hate it when we argue. Not because I fear any permanent damage. We are beyond such things, you and I. But because it is a waste of time. I have squandered time rapaciously. And why not? It was an infinite resource. Until the day you took my hand and asked to see the universe through my eyes. At that moment, time became the most precious of commodities. Its only measure, your every breath. When your eyes close at last, I shall remember the light as it fell across your face in our home on Roska. I shall smile, thinking you but asleep. And then, my time will end. Not because I do not honor your wishes. Because without you, what am I?

INT. *TAZA'S TALE* **- COCKPIT**

Taza's Tale's engines in the background as
we join Seven in the small cockpit. The comms
crackle with static as an anonymous voice comes
through emotionless.

> VOICE:
> ...avoid systems close to the Karzha Belt,
> reports of increased raider activity...
> emergency beacon still active from merchant
> vessel two light-years from the Piko
> system...Romulan warbird detected on course
> to depart the Napiri Sector.

Seven switches off the comms.

> SEVEN:
> Computer, how long before we intercept the
> *Wrath*?

> COMPUTER:
> Eleven minutes and thirty-four seconds on
> current heading.

> SEVEN:
> Maintain course. Computer, set comms to
> record for transmission to the *Tendu*.

> COMPUTER:
> Recording.

> SEVEN:
> Raffi, it's me. I'm sorry. I should have said
> good-bye.
> > (beat)
> But you would have talked me out of it. You'd
> have said it's suicide. I know it isn't. I'm

good at this. Helping people who can't help themselves.

CUE: SEVEN AND RAFFI THEME, SOFTLY

> SEVEN (CONT'D):

It's all I know. All I am. Sometimes, when we're together, I can almost glimpse something in the distance. A possibility. Something different. And it scares the hell out of me.

> (beat)

Computer. Stop recording.

> COMPUTER:

Recording stopped.

Seven sighs deeply.

> SEVEN:

Computer, delete recording.

> COMPUTER:

Recording deleted.

> SEVEN:

Maintain present course.

INT. *WRATH* - HOLDING CELL

Scuffling sounds as Gillan hits the cell floor
and groans.

>   RYNIN:
>   You'll tell me where your wife would have
>   gone, Professor, or this cell is the last
>   place you'll ever see. No Lemniscate to keep
>   you alive now.

Scuffle as Rynin grabs Gillan by the collar and
chokes him.

>   RYNIN (CONT'D):
>   (in close, hissing)
>   My new Romulan Empire will not be grounded
>   in fear and terror. But in order for it to
>   endure, I must endure. I would let you live.
>   Teach me how to use the gift of eternity. But
>   you must tell me where it is!

Gillan's barely conscious now.

Koliva approaches.

>   KOLIVA:
>   My Emperor!

Rynin lets Gillan go.

>   KOLIVA (CONT'D)
>   A ship approaches on an intercept course.
>   Small fighter, single pilot, but weapons hot.

>   RYNIN:
>   So destroy it and stop wasting my time.

>   KOLIVA:
>   Emperor, please...

                    RYNIN:
Go!

                    KOLIVA:
Rynin, I know you didn't find what you wanted
on Roska. But if you kill this man, you'll
never find the eternity you seek.

                    RYNIN:
Think on what I've said, Professor. You knew
her better than anyone. Where would she have
gone? Somewhere in that fragile, decaying
mind, you know the truth. And you will tell
me, one way or the other.
            (to Koliva)
Come. We've a ship to destroy and songs of
victory to sing.

Rynin departs. Koliva opens a comm channel.

                    KOLIVA:
Koliva to surgical bay. Send a medic to the
holding cells at once.

INT. *TAZA'S TALE* **- COCKPIT**
CUE: BATTLE THEME

Deep hum of warp travel. A countdown beeps as the
ship exits warp.

> COMPUTER:
> Exiting warp in 3...2...1...

The hum stops, replaced by the rumble of the
impulse engines.

> SEVEN:
> Scan for target.

> COMPUTER:
> Target acquired.

> SEVEN:
> There you are, Rynin. Computer, switch to
> manual control.

A short beep sequence as the computer complies.

> COMPUTER:
> Manual control initiated.

> SEVEN:
> Let's get a little closer.

Engines flare and the ships whooshes as it pulls
in close behind the *Wrath*. Warning beeps blare.

> COMPUTER:
> Warning, proximity alert.

> SEVEN:
> That's the idea. Charge phasers.

Sound of twin phaser banks humming to life, then
firing, followed by the crackle of the blasts
hitting the *Wrath*'s shields.

COMPUTER:
Enemy shields holding. Enemy arming photon torpedoes.

SEVEN:
Let's swing around in front and say hello.

Engines flare and the ship swooshes again. The warning beeps repeat.

COMPUTER:
Proximity alert. Proximity al—

SEVEN:
Computer, disable proximity alert.

The warning beeps cease.

SEVEN (CONT'D):
That's better.

Seven fires two more phaser blasts, followed by the *Wrath*'s shields crackling.

SEVEN (CONT'D):
Damn. Shields are holding up pretty well for an old warbird.

COMPUTER:
Enemy torpedoes locking on.

SEVEN:
Which is why I'm staying close. They can't fire on me if I stay inside their—

Two heavy blasts come from the *Wrath*.

COMPUTER:
Enemy torpedoes launched.

SEVEN:
Okaaay.

Engines flare and the ship swoops again.

SEVEN (CONT'D):
Deploying countermeasures.

A whine rises in the cockpit, but suddenly fades
like a dying toy.

SEVEN (CONT'D):
Deploy countermeasures!

COMPUTER:
Torpedoes closing.

SEVEN:
Come on!

Seven bashes her fist against the console. The
whine rises again and this time ends in three
quick beeps.

COMPUTER:
Countermeasures deployed.

SEVEN:
Thank you!

Explosions outside the ship as the torpedoes
detonate, but the shock wave rocks the cockpit.

SEVEN (CONT'D):
Maybe a little too close.

COMPUTER:
The enemy ship is hailing us.

SEVEN:
Fine. Open comms.

Rynin's voice booms through the comms.

> RYNIN:
> Seven of Nine? Didn't I kill you in the
> Vendla system?

> SEVEN:
> When you honestly can't remember if you
> killed someone, you might be killing too many
> people, Rynin.

> RYNIN:
> Emperor Rynin.

> SEVEN:
> Since when? I mean, you can call yourself
> whatever you like, but that doesn't make you
> an emperor.

Two more heavy blasts hit Seven's shields.

> SEVEN (CONT'D):
>   (softly)
> Where the hell is that shield emitter?

> COMPUTER:
> Acquiring target.

> SEVEN:
> Acquire faster.
>   (beat)
> Rynin? You still there? I'll make this easy
> for you. Transport Professor Gillan to my
> ship and we can part enemies.

Another blast hits Seven's shields.

> SEVEN (CONT'D):
> Rynin, I'm talking to you, you pathetic
> wannabe emperor.

Seven works her console. Another hit, small
explosion inside the cockpit. Alarm sounds. Seven
silences it.

> SEVEN (CONT'D):
> Where did it all go wrong, Rynin? Mommy
> didn't love you enough? Best friend slept
> with your concubine?

Sound of hard turn, Romulan phasers grazing
Seven's ship.

> RYNIN:
> (to his crew)
> Why is this taking so long?

> SEVEN:
> Must be tough being the bastard son of a dead
> empire.

More beeps and clicks as Seven works her console.

> SEVEN (CONT'D):
> (to herself)
> C'mon. C'mon. Give me my target.

> COMPUTER:
> Target acquired.

> SEVEN:
> Locking phasers.

> RYNIN:
> The day my home world died was the greatest
> day of life. It set me free. Gave me purpose.

> SEVEN:
> FIRE!

Phasers fire. Distant explosion.

                    COMPUTER:
Direct hit.

                     SEVEN:
Close comms. Evasive pattern Seven Alpha
Six. Just keep us clear while I locate the
professor and lock transporters.

Phaser fire, impact and whine of engine.

                    COMPUTER:
Shields compromised. Sixty-two percent and
falling.

                     SEVEN:
Evasive pattern Seven Gamma Three. Come on,
scanners. How hard is it to find the only
person on that ship who isn't a Romulan?

Phasers blast from the *Wrath*. Seven's engines
flare, and the ship whines under pressure as it
swoops away from the *Wrath*.

                    COMPUTER:
Shields disabled.

                     SEVEN:
Just one more pass.

Sound of targeting scanner acquired.

                 SEVEN (CONT'D):
Got him! Computer, engage...

Boom. A direct hit. The hull metal warps from the
blast. The cockpit rattles, control panels break
open and sparks fly, warning sirens blare.

                    COMPUTER:
Critical damage to starboard hull. Life-
support at ninety-two percent and falling.

                    SEVEN:
              (frustrated)
Damn it!
              (beat)
Get us out of here!

                    COMPUTER:
Heading?

                    SEVEN:
The planet! Emergency landing protocol!

A steady roar begins to grow as the ship heads
toward the planet. Engines whining, cockpit
sparking, sirens blaring.

                    COMPUTER:
Inertial dampers engaged. Prepare for
landing.

The roar finally terminates in a massive crash as
the ship hits the surface and skids, kicking up
rubble and shedding broken pieces of hull before
it finally groans to a stop. Quiet, but for soft
beeping from the cockpit. Seven groans and shifts
in her seat, recovering.

                    SEVEN:
Damn it, Raffi...
              (winces)
Ow!
              (sighs)
...you were right.

ACT THREE

ACT THREE

EXT. *U.S.S. NIGHTINGALE* - **SURFACE**
CUE: ADVENTURE THEME

Raffi and Deet stand outside the downed
Federation *Starship Nightingale*.

She's a smaller science vessel, but she's the
most beautiful thing Raffi has seen since this
whole mess started.

> DEET:
> What do you think?

> RAFFI:
> I think you could get in huge trouble for
> hiding a Starfleet ship here. The *U.S.S.*
> *Nightingale*. Wow. Do you know what happened
> to her? You guys didn't bring her down, did
> you?

Raffi and Deet board the ship.

> DEET:
> She was found adrift and towed here a few
> years ago. The Rangers have made use of some
> of her internal systems, but I think she can
> still fly.

> RAFFI:
> Primary power is down. Let's see if the
> backup generator feels like turning on.

Sound of screeching metal quickly subsides into
the gentle hum of Starfleet ship ambience.

> RAFFI (CONT'D):
> Got it. Main computer is coming online.

> DEET:
> This isn't a battleship, is it?

> RAFFI:

Hmm? No. Science vessel. But all Starfleet ships are always battle ready. She's got phasers, maybe even a few torpedoes.
>   (beat)

Aha! Way more important, she's got a functioning communications array. Which means someone out there who has eyes on Rynin can tell me— No. You know what? No. She went after him alone. She wants to play it that way? Fine.

Deet bangs on something metal.

> DEET:

Devanetian chocolate milk!

> RAFFI:

Whoa, whoa, what are you doing?

> DEET:

This is a replicator, is it not?

> RAFFI:

Yeah.

> DEET:

So it can make anything I want.

> RAFFI:

Oh, no, honey. It can make anything it's programmed to make. Food, clothing, some basic medical supplies.

Deet addresses the replicator.

> DEET:

Chocolate milk?

Swirling sound of replicator.

                    RAFFI:
There you go.

                    DEET:
It's like magic.

                    RAFFI:
It's really not.

A pause.

                    DEET:
Can the *Nightingale* fly again?

                    RAFFI:
It'll take work. But she's not in bad shape.

                    DEET:
We should go after Seven.

                    RAFFI:
Oh, no. No, no. If I use this ship for
anything, it'll be to get the hell out of here.

                    DEET:
We should go after Seven.

                    RAFFI:
Seven shouldn't have left.

CUE: SEVEN AND RAFFI THEME

                    DEET:
We should find her, and you should tell her
that. She is different since she met you. You
upset her. In a good way.

                    RAFFI:
She doesn't need me to save her. She made
that very clear yesterday. As of now, I am
officially out of the saving-Seven business.

                    DEET:
And she upsets you. That is also good.

                    RAFFI:
Wait, how is she different, exactly?

                    DEET:
She laughs with you. When you are not
upsetting her. I don't remember hearing her
laugh before.

                    RAFFI:
Even if that's true, we can't fly this thing
alone.

                    DEET:
Wouldn't have to.

                    RAFFI:
What do you mean?

                    DEET:
I would like to join Starfleet.

                    RAFFI:
What?

                    DEET:
Hyro should join Starfleet as well. And we
should save Seven so that you can continue to
upset each other.

INT. PROFESSOR'S CABIN

Seven enters.

> SEVEN:
> Huh. Congratulations, Professor. Your home is
> now an archeological ruin. Courtesy of Rynin,
> I presume.
> >(beat)
> So this is why Rynin brought you here. And
> you were still alive a few hours ago, which
> means whatever Rynin wants, he doesn't have
> it yet.
> >(beat)
> You were the most important thing on Ebla.
> But why?

Seven dusts off a surface. Taps a panel. It comes
to life with the sound of a welcoming chime. Its
voice is that of a kind, older human female—Helena.

> COMPUTER:
> Good evening, my love. How can I help you?

> SEVEN:
> >(clears her throat)
> Um, hello?

> COMPUTER:
> Unable to authenticate voice print.

> SEVEN:
> I know. You don't know me. But I'm trying
> to help Professor Gillan. Can you assist me
> anyway?

> COMPUTER:
> Professor Gillan is unavailable at this time.
> Please return—

> SEVEN:

Are there any other authentication protocols
active?

> COMPUTER:

Protocols enabled include biometric, genetic
sequence, passcode, and vocal verification.

> SEVEN:

Hang on.

Seven pulls Helena's gloves out of her pocket and
puts one on her hand.

> SEVEN (CONT'D):

Computer, scan this glove for genetic
sequence verification.

Sound of scan and soft chime.

> COMPUTER:

Identity authenticated. Helena Gillan. Access
granted.

> SEVEN:

Show me the last records you have in your
database including Professor Gillan and
Helena.

> COMPUTER:

The following files were transmitted to
archive over subspace relays in 2386 and have
not been reviewed or verified.

> SEVEN:

That's okay. Show me anyway.

A short pause, then sounds of Helena's laughter
in exterior on Gorvan VI sitting around a
campfire.

HELENA:

Oh, not now. Please.

Note that at this time in his life, Gillan was
sane.

GILLAN:

This is for posterity.

HELENA:

I'm exhausted. And I look terrible.

GILLAN:

You look as lovely as the day we met.
          (beat)
Now. Day sixteen, Gorvan VI. Primary site,
dwelling foundation, kitchen.

HELENA:

I still think it was the latrine.

GILLAN:

Had I thought to visit here two thousand
years ago, I might have been able to settle
this. As it is, I believe these fragments
represent a Mid-Calabrian-era warming vessel.

HELENA:

You're going to have to go soon. I wish we'd
had more time.

GILLAN:

Oh, we'll return. Don't worry. Once the nova
wave passes, things will settle down and
I'll prove to you that this was, in fact, a
kitchen.

HELENA:

I want you to promise me something.

                    GILLAN:
Anything, love.

                    HELENA:
When the officers return next week for the
final evacuations, you'll go with them.

                    GILLAN:
They can't force us, you know.

                    HELENA:
We're not all immortal, darling.

Gillan pulls a metal necklace and amulet from
around his neck.

                    GILLAN:
Not this again. Here, take it. I don't want
it anymore.

                    HELENA:
The Lemniscate is a gift. Your gift. We both
know I won't live forever. You have to go on,
without me.

                    GILLAN:
Take it. Without you, eternity would be
unbearable.

                    SEVEN:
Computer, pause recording. Define
"Lemniscate."

                    COMPUTER:
In algebraic geometry, a lemniscate is any
set of figure-eight-shaped curves.

                    SEVEN:
Infinity? Eternity?
          (Seven gets it)
You weren't just naturally long-lived, were

you, Professor? That object you kept around
your neck, the Lemniscate, extended your
life.
>   (beat)
That's what Rynin wants. But you don't have
it anymore, do you? You gave it to her.
>   (beat)
Computer, resume recording.

>   HELENA:
We both know I'm never leaving this planet.

>   GILLAN:
You're just tired, my love. A good night's
sleep is all you need.

>   HELENA:
I know you don't want to see it. But, darling—

>   GILLAN:
Take it. Just take the damn thing.

>   HELENA:
No. Absolutely not. I won't watch you die, my
love. And without it, you would, wouldn't you?

>   GILLAN:
I don't know. It didn't come with an
instruction manual. I have no idea what
happens to me without it. I never had cause
to test it.

>   SEVEN:
End playback. Damn it. Raffi was right again.

CUE: ADVENTURE THEME

Seven runs out of the house.

EXT. ROSKA - NIGHT

Seven attempts to start her ship's engine. It whines and sputters.

> SEVEN:
> Come on, come on. I've rerouted everything to the engines. I've sealed the breaches. Diagnostics are clean. I know you can do this. You have to do this.

Another attempt. This time it clicks and the engine hums to life.

> SEVEN (CONT'D):
> Yes! Transmit encoded message on all Fenris channels. *Taza's Tale* is en route to Gorvan VI. Anyone in range, rendezvous at these coordinates.
> (beat)
> Send transmission.

> COMPUTER:
> Transmission sent.

> SEVEN:
> Let's go.

Seven's ship launches from the surface of Roska.

CUE: ADVENTURE THEME

INT. *WRATH* **- BRIG**

Gillan sits inside the *Wrath*'s holding cell.

An electric crackle as the cell's force field
lowers.

> GILLAN:
> (fearful, weak)
> N-no...I've told you...home is wherever
> she...

> KOLIVA:
> (gentle)
> Shhh. I'm not going to hurt you. Here,
> something for the pain.

The hiss of a hypospray.

> GILLAN:
> Yes...thank you...

> KOLIVA:
> I can help you, but the emperor will not
> wait forever. You must tell him where the
> Lemniscate is. He won't stop hurting you
> until you do.

> GILLAN:
> Fear is for those who have something to lose,
> my dear.

> KOLIVA:
> He will kill you.

> GILLAN:
> I have already lived more life than most
> and all that I care to. The soup here is
> terrible, by the way.

                         KOLIVA:
              (gently)
          But Helena's was delicious?

CUE: LOVE LETTER THEME

                         GILLAN:
          Exquisite.

                         KOLIVA:
          My father used to make a red vine paste in
          broth whenever I wasn't feeling well. I
          hadn't thought of that in years.

                         GILLAN:
          But the memory comforts you.

                         KOLIVA:
          I suppose.

                         GILLAN:
          Those are the ones you must recall as often
          as possible. They'll keep you warm in the
          coldest universe.

                         KOLIVA:
          Like Helena's soup.

                         GILLAN:
          Mmm. I can still taste it.

                         KOLIVA:
          Tell me more about her.

CUE: RYNIN'S THEME

INT. *WRATH* - RYNIN'S QUARTERS

Rynin is sleeping. The door chimes.

> RYNIN:
>> (waking, annoyed)
>
> Enter!

Door opens. Koliva enters.

> KOLIVA:
>
> My Emperor. A ship matching Seven of Nine's
> has been reported en route to Gorvan VI.

> RYNIN:
>
> She survived? Didn't our sensors show her
> crashing into Roska? I become less confident
> in my crew's abilities by the hour.
>> (beat)
>
> You wish to make an example of her? Set a
> pursuit course?

> KOLIVA:
>
> I was speaking to the professor—

> RYNIN:
>
> Who gave you permission to interrogate the
> prisoner?

> KOLIVA:
>> (quickly)
>
> I asked him about his wife. He said they were
> working on a dig site on Gorvan VI before
> they were evacuated.

> RYNIN:
>
> But he has no idea where she went?

                         KOLIVA:
Sir. Starfleet's public records of all
evacuees from Gorvan VI do not include her
name. I don't think she ever left there,
except in his heart.

Rynin laughs.

                         RYNIN:
What could you know of his heart? Still, if
the Ranger is headed there, she has cause.
          (beat)
If you are right, you will be well rewarded
for this in the new empire. Alter course
at once.

INT. *NIGHTINGALE* - BRIDGE
CUE: CHEERFUL CLASSICAL MUSIC

We find Raffi and Hyro mid-conversation. Deet
listens.

> HYRO:
> It's out of the question! We are Fenris
> Rangers. And there's a reason for that. None
> of us ever had the slightest interest in
> joining Starfleet.

> RAFFI:
> Nobody is swearing any oaths. All we're asking
> is for a skeleton crew to man critical stations
> for a couple of days at the most. *Tendu* can't
> take on Rynin, but *Nightingale* can.

> HYRO:
> This ship is barely holding orbit. It's no
> threat to Rynin.

> RAFFI:
> No, it isn't. But the Federation is. He
> wants to be the new emperor, right? He needs
> legitimacy for that. He can kill individual
> operatives, but crossing a Starfleet vessel
> would demand a response. He doesn't want
> a war with the Federation. They'll never
> recognize his authority after that.

> HYRO:
> They'll never recognize it now.

> RAFFI:
> You know that. And I know that. But I'll bet
> all the money in your pocket Rynin doesn't.

                        HYRO:
    It's a huge gamble.

                        RAFFI:
    That's my favorite kind.

Suddenly, red alert klaxons wail.

                        HYRO:
    What the...?

                        RAFFI:
    Deet?!

The red alert klaxon is shut off.

                        DEET:
    Oops. Sorry. I just wanted to know what it
    sounds like.

Raffi sighs audibly.

                        DEET:
    Also, I've intercepted a transmission from
    Seven. She's going to Gorvan VI.

                        RAFFI:
    Did she say why?

                        DEET:
    Does it matter?

                        RAFFI:
    No. You're the best, Deet. Plot a course at
    our best-possible warp speed.

                        HYRO:
    Wait a minute. Since when do you speak
    Federation Standard?

RAFFI:
(covers quickly)
Universal translators are built into the comm
systems of every Starfleet ship. But I'll
tear it out with my bare hands if you'll do
this with me.

HYRO:
I would be the captain?

RAFFI:
How do you look in red?

HYRO:
No uniforms!

RAFFI:
Hyro, for this to work, we have to sell it.
Think of it as an undercover mission. You
Rangers ever do those?

HYRO:
(momentarily considering it)
Intrigue. Spy craft. Misinformalizing.

RAFFI:
Yeah, all of that. Plus, when we're done,
we file off the registry numbers, and the
Rangers have themselves another ship to help
evacuate Ebla.
(beat)
Bring me your best and let's get you guys
sworn into Starfleet.

HYRO:
You said...!

                    RAFFI:
I'm kidding. Ha-ha-ha, I'm kidding! But I
will need your sizes.

                    HYRO:
No uniforms.

                    RAFFI:
Big ship. All yours.

CUE: ADVENTURE THEME

INT. *WRATH* - BRIDGE

Rynin, Gillan, and Koliva enter.

> RYNIN:
> Maintain a lock on my signal while I'm on the
> surface.

> KOLIVA:
> Yes, Emperor.

> CENTURIAN:
> My Emperor, there is no sign of the Fenris
> Ranger. But she could be waiting in ambush.

> RYNIN:
> I would be disappointed in her if she wasn't.
> She's most likely hiding in the unstable
> atmospherics at the northern pole. Maintain
> this orbit, Koliva. But if the Ranger makes
> her move, destroy her.

> RYNIN (CONT'D):
> I'll be back from the surface soon enough.

> KOLIVA:
> What about the professor?

> GILLAN:
> Don't worry about me, my dear. I won't be
> returning from this little excursion. And
> if I may say, I would encourage you to seek
> out alternative employment at the earliest
> opportunity. I've known more than a few
> madmen in my day. They don't change.

> RYNIN:
> Shut up, old man.

Scuffling as Rynin drags Gillan up onto the transporter pads.

                    RYNIN (CONT'D):
     Commence transport.

                    KOLIVA:
     Yes, my Emperor.

The transporter beams Rynin and Gillan out. It continues...

EXT. GORVAN VI

...As the two of them arrive on the surface of
Gorvan VI. The transporter hum fades, replaced
by the sound of hell: swirling winds, crumbling
rocks, the ground shaking from constant
earthquakes. Volcanoes rumble in the distance.

Rynin and Gillan both cough and gasp in the
sulfuric air.

> GILLAN:
> This can't be right.

> RYNIN:
> Gorvan's orbit around its main star was
> altered by the nova. It's changed since
> you were last here. But these were the
> coordinates where you were found and
> evacuated.

> GILLAN:
> I'm so sorry to disappoint you, my dear. You
> didn't want me to die here as well, but I
> don't really mind.

> RYNIN:
> You left her here. And the Lemniscate with
> her, so she would survive. Where is she?

> GILLAN:
> This way.

The cacophony continues. Rynin and Gillan
grunt as they make their way across the rocky
landscape. Their footsteps occasionally slip,
causing ground to give way.

GILLAN (CONT'D):
Careful! This is quite unstable.

RYNIN:
Your concern is touching, old man.
(beat)
Why have you stopped?

Gillan falls to his knees and begins to weep.

GILLAN:
(ignoring him)
Oh, my love. My dearest love.

RYNIN:
What is this?

The click and whine of a phaser rifle powering up. Seven steps out from a cove.

SEVEN:
It's a grave, you son of a bitch.

INT. *WRATH* - BRIDGE

> CENTURIAN:
> Koliva, there's a ship incoming.

> KOLIVA:
> Lock weapons and fire the moment Seven of
> Nine is in range.

> CENTURIAN:
> Forgive me, but it's a Starfleet vessel!

> KOLIVA:
> Starfleet has no vessels in this area. At
> least not officially.

> CENTURIAN:
> They're hailing us!

> KOLIVA:
> Let's hear it.

> RAFFI:
> (over comms)
> Romulan vessel, this is Captain Raffaela
> Musiker of the Federation *Starship
> Nightingale*. This entire sector is under
> Federation protection pending the resolution
> of certain territorial disputes. Break orbit
> and depart immediately or we will open fire.

> KOLIVA:
> Raise shields! All hands to batt—

A quick rising swoosh as a photon torpedo
arrives, followed by a massive boom as it hits
the *Wrath*. The hull shudders, crew members shout,
sparks fly, and fires break out on the bridge.

INT. *NIGHTINGALE* - BRIDGE
CUE: OPERATIC MUSIC

RAFFI:
NOT NOW, DEET!

Music abruptly shuts off.

RAFFI (CONT'D):
Why the hell did you fire, Hyro?

HYRO:
We're not here to take them into custody,
or whatever Starfleet does. We're here to
destroy them.

RAFFI:
The professor could still be on board.

DEET:
Sensors show three life signs on the
surface.

RAFFI:
Shit. I'm going down there. Don't do anything
stupid while I'm gone.

HYRO:
Aren't you going to say it?

RAFFI:
Say what? Oh. Right. Hyro, the conn is yours.
And it better be in one piece when I get
back.

HYRO:
Of course, Captain.

Doors open and close.

HYRO (CONT'D):

My, this chair is comfortable. Right. Shields
up. Charge phaser banks. Load torpedoes.
That's right, isn't it? Yes. That's right.
> (beat)

As you were, Deet.

CUE: OPERATIC SONG RESUMES

EXT. GORVAN IV - GRAVESIDE
BACK ON THE HELLISH SURFACE OF THE PLANET

Seven has her rifle trained on Rynin as Gillan looks on. They shout to be heard over the planetary chaos.

> SEVEN:
> Let him go, Rynin.

> GILLAN:
> (confused)
> Helena?

> RYNIN:
> He's not going anywhere until I have the Lemniscate!

Rynin approaches Seven.

> SEVEN:
> Stay back, Rynin!

> RYNIN:
> (approaching)
> You know where it is, don't you, Ranger? Tell me...

> SEVEN:
> I'm warning you—!

Rynin yells as he jumps at Seven. She fires, hitting him in the leg. He hits the ground and cries out in pain.

> SEVEN (CONT'D):
> The next shot'll be higher than your knee, Rynin!
> (to Gillan)
> Professor, we need to get out of—

GILLAN:
No! Seven, watch there! He's—

Rynin yells as he heaves himself up and lunges at
Seven. He knocks her rifle out of her hands and
it skitters away against the rocks.

Seven gasps as Rynin gets her in a choke hold.

RYNIN:
(straining)
Give me...what is mine...

Seven struggles for air.

RYNIN (CONT'D):
Or you die...on this wretched rock...

Seven yells as she frees herself from Rynin,
spinning away. They fight, each one grunting with
exertion, each one landing hits on the other.

GILLAN:
Stop it, both of you!

The fight continues.

RYNIN:
Enough!

Rynin yells and strikes Seven, sending her flat
on her back with a thump on the rocky surface.

GILLAN:
Seven!

RYNIN:
We'll make sure you're dead this time.

Suddenly a Starfleet transporter effect sounds.
Raffi materializes on the scene.

                    RAFFI:
Rynin!!

                    RYNIN:
Who are you?

                    RAFFI:
Acting Captain Raffaela Musiker of the
Federation *Starship Nightingale*.

Zap, zap!

Raffi stuns Rynin with a flurry of phaser shots.
He drops to the ground with a thud.

                RAFFI (CONT'D):
And I'm not here for your bullshit.

Raffi moves to secure Rynin, clamping manacles
around Rynin's wrists.

                RAFFI (CONT'D):
Unconscious, hands secured behind his back.
Hard for him to misbehave now.

                    SEVEN:
Raffi...how...?

Raffi turns to Seven, pissed.

                    RAFFI:
What did I tell you? He had you dead to
rights just now.

                    SEVEN:
I know. You were right. I'm sorry.

                    RAFFI:
You should be.
            (beat)
How could you just leave me like that?

SEVEN:
I thought I could handle it.

RAFFI:
We've been over the math. Tiny ship. Warbird. You lose.

SEVEN:
That's not what I'm talking about.

RAFFI:
Oh.

SEVEN:
You're a lot, Raffi. You're willing to go all in here. And I don't know if I can do that—yet.

RAFFI:
So we have a conversation. That's what people do when they're scared and they care about each other.

SEVEN:
That's when I usually run.

The sound of digging. Hands scratching the ground, dirt and pebbles scattering.

GILLAN:
My love, oh, my dearest love...

SEVEN:
Professor, what...
            (winces in pain)
...what are you doing?

More digging as the professor continues.

GILLAN:
She wanted us to leave when the first ships came. But I was so certain she would be fine.

SEVEN:
Professor, it's okay.

GILLAN:
She wasn't fine. And I refused to see it. I'd
always known when the time came that I would
give it to her. But she wouldn't allow it.
And when I woke that morning, she was already
gone. It was too late.

The scratching of metal and shifting of dirt as
Gillan pulls something from the ground. It's two
pieces of an amulet, the same amulet Seven saw in
the holovid on Roska.

RAFFI:
What is that? Some kind of necklace?

SEVEN:
Professor, is that the Lemniscate?

RAFFI:
Lemnis-what?

SEVEN:
It's what Rynin was after. It's—

GILLAN:
It bestows eternal life on the one who wears
it. I know, it sounds like a wondrous gift.
For a historian, an unimaginable boon. It was
given to me by a traveler...

RAFFI:
Why would anyone give up eternal life?

GILLAN:
Because he came to realize, as I did, that
it is as much a curse as a blessing. Family,
friends, lovers living and dying while you

cannot. It was only once I met Helena that I understood why he gave it away.

> SEVEN:
> She died. So you broke it, and buried it with her.

> GILLAN:
> (breaking down)
> Oh, Helena...Oh, my love...

Seven puts her arms around Gillan.

> SEVEN:
> It's all right, Professor. Shh. It's all right now.

> RAFFI:
> Honey, we really have to get off this planet.

> SEVEN:
> (gently to the professor)
> Are you ready?

> GILLAN:
> I am.

> RAFFI:
> Musiker to *Nightingale*. Four to beam up.

INT. *NIGHTINGALE* - BRIDGE - LATER
CUE: ROCK MUSIC

Seven and Raffi enter the bridge.

                    DEET:
Captain on the bridge.

                    HYRO:
I am indeed.

                    RAFFI:
No, I'm the captain. Starfleet ships don't
have more than one captain on them at a time.

                    HYRO:
What if something happens to the captain?

                    SEVEN:
That's what first officers are for.

                    HYRO:
Ridiculous. You should have at least two
captains. The way you all run through
officers these days...

                    SEVEN:
Hyro!

                    HYRO:
Feeling better now, Seven? Ready to start
evacuating Ebla at long last?

                    SEVEN:
Yes. And by the way, you look spectacular in
uniform.

                    DEET:
They're oddly quite comfortable.

RAFFI:

What happened?

HYRO:

Our first shot took out their shields. The
second, their weapons. After that a very
frightened woman named Koliva offered her
surrender, which I graciously accepted. I then
sent a message to any Starfleet ship in the
area to take custody of the *Wrath*. Terribly
officious young man on something called the
U.S.S. Ginsburg advised that they have altered
course and should be here within the hour.

SEVEN:

So how do you like Starfleet now?

HYRO:

At a distance, just as you do, Seven.

RAFFI:

Not bad, Hyro. Not bad at all.

HYRO:

Rynin?

RAFFI:

Brig.

HYRO:

The professor?

SEVEN:

Sickbay.

HYRO:

We don't have staff down there.

SEVEN:

No, but you do have an EMH.

                    HYRO:
What's that?

                    SEVEN:
A program we should seriously think about
acquiring.

                    RAFFI:
I better call the *Ginsburg* and let them know
what to expect when they get here.

                    HYRO:
The ship is still mine, isn't it? I've grown
rather fond of her.

                    RAFFI:
What ship are you talking about? I certainly
never saw a Starfleet ship out here.

Raffi exits.

                    SEVEN:
Look at the two of you, almost getting along.

                    HYRO:
Honestly, you should watch your back. I think
she's quite taken with me.

INT. PROFESSOR'S QUARTERS - LATER
CUE: LOVE LETTER THEME

Seven enters to find the professor resting. He
is, finally, more clear of mind.

> GILLAN:
> Ah, my dear, there you are.

> SEVEN:
> Feeling better?

> GILLAN:
> Much. Yes, I think so.

> SEVEN:
> I have something for you.

> GILLAN:
> Ah, my letters. Kept them all these years,
> did you?

> SEVEN:
> I spend a lot of time alone out here. They've
> kept me company. I thought you might want
> them back.

> GILLAN:
> No. That's all right. Keep them. They should
> be of use to someone. Helena would have liked
> that.

> SEVEN:
> The love you had—have—for her. It's quite
> something.

> GILLAN:
> Everyone should be so blessed.

SEVEN:
It's rare, at least in my experience.
Difficult to find.

GILLAN:
Oh, no, no, my dear. Not at all. Love is
essential and common, a base drive that
brings us together so our species can
endure. What Helena and I had was built over
a lifetime, moment by moment, and endures
because whenever I return to those precious
moments, I live within them again with
Helena.

SEVEN:
A certain slant of light.

GILLAN:
Precisely. It's not something you find, Miss
Seven. It's something you create.

EXT. RAFFI'S PORCH - NIGHT - A MONTH LATER
CUE: I'LL ALWAYS BE WAITING

>   RECORD PLAYS:
> *I'll always be waiting, I just can't pretend,*
> *no matter where, no matter when, until I see*
> *you again...*

Raffi reads the last letter.

>   RAFFI:
> I almost rejected his offer. Tempting as it
> was to know that I would never die unless I
> chose to part with the Lemniscate, it was
> also terrifying. When eternity yawns before
> you, it becomes impossible to conceive
> something so vast. To grasp it is to be
> suffocated by it. You taught me to breathe,
> dear one. To live in each breath. You make
> eternity bearable.

The porch door opens, and Seven joins Raffi.

>   RAFFI:
> You're right. The professor writes a hell of
> a love letter.

Seven pours wine.

>   SEVEN:
> To a job well done.

They clink glasses.

>   RAFFI:
> I can't remember the last time I was this
> tired.

>   SEVEN:
> You just moved the history of an entire

civilization across a dozen sectors and
rebuilt it. You should be tired.

                    RAFFI:
But also...great. You know?

                    SEVEN:
I do.
          (beat)
There's plenty more where that came from.

                    RAFFI:
The wine?

                    SEVEN:
The work.

CUE: SEVEN AND RAFFI THEME

                    RAFFI:
Seven—

                    SEVEN:
Just—let me say this.

                    RAFFI:
Okay.

                    SEVEN:
It's been years since I sat still long enough
to even think about—you know.

                    RAFFI:
I think I do.

                    SEVEN:
I find commitment...

                    RAFFI:
Suffocating?

SEVEN:

Baffling.

Raffi laughs.

SEVEN (CONT'D):
But it would be nice to have—no—to create
something worth sacrificing eternity for.

RAFFI:
It would.

SEVEN:
So...

RAFFI:
JL reached out while we were gone.

SEVEN:
Oh.

RAFFI:
He's got a job for me. I don't know how he
did it, but they want me back.

SEVEN:
Starfleet?

RAFFI:
Yeah.

SEVEN:
The love that dies hard.

RAFFI:
Yeah.

SEVEN:
You're sure?

                    RAFFI:
I am. I know what I want here. I'm not sure
you do, yet. And that's okay. There's no
rush.
           (beat)
What these two people had, Gillan and Helena,
takes commitment. And for that, you have to
at least believe it's possible.

                    SEVEN:
I'm willing to at least suspend my disbelief.

                    RAFFI:
So let that be enough, for now. We don't have
to figure it all out tonight. You know where
I am and where I'll be.

                    SEVEN:
So we go slow. One moment at a time.

                    RAFFI:
Mmm-hm.

                    SEVEN:
I can do that.

Seven kisses Raffi tenderly.

                    RAFFI:
           (suddenly excited)
Oh! By the way.

                    SEVEN:
You're killing this moment. You do realize
that.

                    RAFFI:
I do. But this is good. JL made good on his
promise. He found you a ship.

SEVEN:

What?

RAFFI:

Hyro keeps the *Nightingale*. Let Deet have the *Tendu*.

SEVEN:

Picard is giving me a ship?

RAFFI:

Not Picard. But sort of by way of Picard.

SEVEN:

Who?

RAFFI:

See now, I just want you to live with the mystery a little bit longer.

SEVEN:

Raffi!

CUE: SEVEN AND RAFFI THEME

> *I'll always be waiting*
> *I just can't pretend*
> *No matter where*
> *No matter when*
> *Until I see you again*

END

Kirsten Beyer was a cocreator of the acclaimed hit Paramount+ series *Star Trek: Picard*, where she served as writer and supervising producer for season one and a coexecutive producer for season two. She has also written and produced *Star Trek: Discovery* and is currently a coexecutive producer on *Star Trek: Strange New Worlds*. She is the *New York Times* bestselling author of the last ten *Star Trek: Voyager* novels, including 2020's *To Lose the Earth*, for which she was the narrator of the audiobook edition. She contributed the short story "Isabo's Shirt" to *Star Trek: Voyager: Distant Shores Anthology*. In 2006, Kirsten appeared at Hollywood's Unknown Theater in their productions of *Johnson Over Jordan*, *This Old Planet*, and Harold Pinter's *The Hothouse*, which the *Los Angeles Times* called "unmissable." She lives in Los Angeles.

Mike Johnson is a *New York Times* bestselling writer of comics, games, and animation. Since 2015, he has worked as a writer and creative consultant for ViacomCBS on *Star Trek* games and interactive projects. His work on the *Star Trek* franchise began in 2009 with *Star Trek: Countdown*, the comics prequel to the blockbuster film *Star Trek* directed by J. J. Abrams. Since then, Johnson has written and cowritten the most *Star Trek* comics in the franchise's history. His other credits include *Superman/Batman*, *Supergirl*, and *Earth 2* for DC Comics, *Transformers* for IDW Publishing, and *Ei8ht* from Dark Horse Comics. He also wrote for the Emmy Award–winning animated show *Transformers: Prime*. Johnson previously worked in film and TV development for writers/producers Alex Kurtzman and Roberto Orci.